Mermaidens

Mermaidens
Copyright © 2022 Knight Writing Press
Additional copyright information for individual works provided at the end of this
publication.

Enrapturing Tales is an imprint of:

Knight Writing Press
PMB # 162
13009 S. Parker Rd.
Parker CO 80134
knightwritingpress.com
KnightWritingPress@gmail.com

Cover Art and Cover Design © 2022 Knight Writing Press

Interior Art © 2022 Knight Writing Press

Additional Copyright Information can be found on page 261

Interior Book Design and eBook Design by Knight Writing Press

Editor Sam Knight

First Publication September 2022

Paperback ISBN-13: 978-1-62869-057-6
eBook ISBN-13: 978-1-62869-058-3

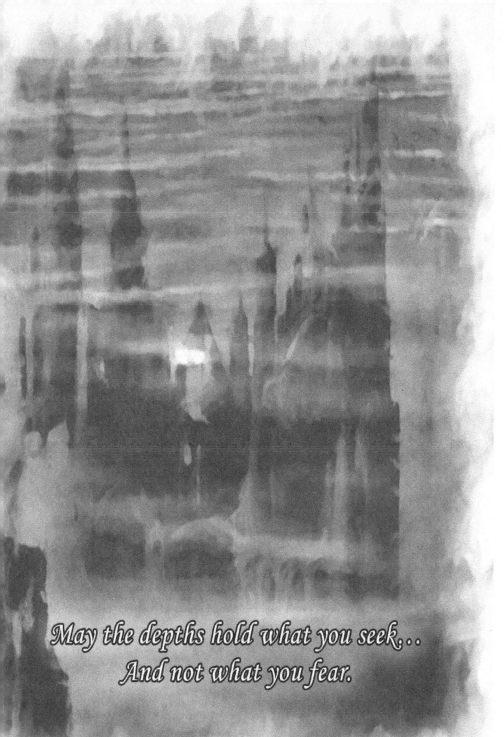

May the depths hold what you seek...
And not what you fear.

Table of Contents

A Note from the Editor

*M*ermaids, in fact Mer people in general, are much like humans in that some are the nicest, kindest, most caring beings anyone could ever hope to meet, while others... Well, let's just say every good story needs a villain, shall we?

The seas run deep, and the deeper you go, the darker they get. There is a reason the phrase is "sinking into the depths of..."

This anthology contains some stories that go into the depths, literally and figuratively.

While I, personally, do not consider any of these stories to have gone too far into that dark abyss, some of them are tinged a bit blue, fading toward black. Some are a bit disturbing. Some deal with adult themes, and some are about violence, and some have curse words.

Most of these stories have mild language, but not all of them do. Most do not contain moral or ethical dilemmas, but some do. Most are not about terrible things, but some of them are.

Though I think the chances anyone will regret reading any of these stories are slight, I feel I should caution those who feel they need warnings.

If that is you, then, just as though you were getting ready to dive off of a cliff and into the sea, I suggest you indulge in careful consideration before you enter this anthology. Consider yourself warned.

If that is not you, if you already know you would jump... Well, you should consider yourself warned as well. There are often rocks at the bottom of the cliffs...and shipwrecks.

-Sam Knight
August 6th, 2022

Where the Wind Blows the Water

by

Matthew F. Amati

Where the Wind Blows the Water

*M*er-moppets with sea-wet hair embraced their mother in a swirl of bubbles. "Tell us the story about Father! How did Father come to live with us?"

Their mother laughed. "Oh, children. Your father was not born of mer-folk. He comes from the far-off heights of Land!"

"And is there no water on Land? And do no schools of fish float by?"

"Your father hails from a human town. Isn't that right, dear?"

Their father grinned, and the children knew it was true.

"And why did Father come to live with us?"

"He was lonely. Isn't that right, my love?"

Father said nothing, only smiled.

"Well, children. Your father…

…was a fisherman. He lived by himself, in a house grimy as a barnacle's bottom. His fire was always going out. He ate his dinners cold with the eyes still on.

One day, a ship docked in the town. The *Texarkana*, westbound out of Southend. The captain hung handbills all over town.

LONELY MEN! FIND YOURSELF A SEA WIFE!

Your father was curious. "What," he asked aloud, "is a Sea Wife?"

An old woman laughed.

"A Sea Wife? A woman of the waters, my friend. A spirit of the deeps, a phantom of the waves, a sweeper of coral-gabled caves. Tempt her to your boat, she'll be your wife for life. Lovely as the dawn salt spray! Eyes like the maelstrom's mystery! Hair like…"

"Like seaweed?" your father wanted to know.

The crone made a face. "Who would want that? No, her hair is like anyone else's hair, once it dries a bit."

The crone leaned close. Your father smelt her breath like rotten clams.

"Think about having your own Sea Wife, sir! A woman who would even love a brute face like your own. A woman to be yours forever."

Your father imagined his Sea Wife. In his kitchen, frying sprats. On his doorstep, sweeping. In his bed, waiting, eyes languorous as the depths of tidal eddies…

"Did he know his Sea Wife would be you, Mother?"

Their mother laughed. Bubbles whirled round. "Of course not. Not at that time. We hadn't met. Had we, dear?"

Father smiled.

Your father signed on board as coxswain, took his berth. The *Texarkana* sailed, in search of Sea Wives! Twelve crew, all rough as rocks, all lonely as guano-dotted crags. All looking to find their loves amid the foam-haired salt-sea spray. Just imagine, children!

Sea-life was hard. Weevils spawned in the ship's biscuit. The biscuit was so tough, the men dissolved it in rum. They had to fight hard and bloody with drunk weevils.

The world of ships was full of unfamiliar words: spar, haws, gaffles, jub, burrmeister, flab line, spinnacle, cassowary, geep. What to make of a command like "Hard abaft the gubbins, men! Flay diligently the aft gumbuckle!" Your father didn't have a clue. He spent the voyage hiding in barrels, reading castoff bibles that held dangerous misprints.

The *Texarkana* sailed past the 180th Meridian. It discovered a little-known 181st Meridian, and many more beyond that. As the crew sailed past where the world ought to have ended, clouds passed from the moon. The North Star set, a thing it had never done before.

As the fires of sunrise boiled World's-End-Waters, the men demanded "Captain! When do we get our Sea Wives?"

"Now," the captain told them. "Now! Your Sea Wives await."

The men ran to the railings.

The captain raised a peculiar large shell to his lips. He called: "Maidens of the deep! I have returned with your Land Husbands!"

"And did Father come to us then?"

"He did! Languorous, slender, persuasive arms pulled him over the port side, into the waiting waters. And your father found himself looking into my very own blue eyes, mysterious as the throats of whirlpools.

"And in the chambers of the sea we met. And under the waves we wed."

"Is supper ready, Mother?"

"Yes, my loves."

"And will Father be having supper?"

Father stretched akimbo in a corner of the cave. His grin was fixed, as always. His jaw was bleached bone. Little fishes swam in and out of his empty eyes.

"Oh, my spawnlings. Your father takes his supper cold with the eyes still on. Of his bones are coral made.

"Pour him eternally his infinite draught of sea."

About the Author

Matthew F. Amati was born in Chicago but was asked to leave soon after. He lives by a canal in Madison, Wisconsin and plays the 5-string banjo. Over 40 of his short stories have appeared in various online and print publications. His novel *Loompaland* is available from places online that sell books.

You can find his collected works on his diffidently-updated website www.mattamati.com.

Coquillages

by

Bridget Day

Coquillages

*F*inn hurried down to the sea after supper, still in his shorts and long socks. The left sock had a nasty tear in it that would send Mabel into a fit if she spotted it. He decided to hide this pair in the box at the back of his wardrobe, where he squirreled his treasures away, until he could dispose of them later.

There were several important items in Finn's makeshift rucksack as he clambered down over the rocky coast. (Another thing that would make his governess wild with worry: her nine-year-old ward climbing this particularly treacherous path down to the shore by himself). The inventory of his precious cargo included three flaky rolls straight from the kitchen and two books that Finn had already read cover to cover, twice. The closer he got to the crash of the waves, the giddier he felt. The salt stung his cheeks, and he turned his face up into the wind to meet it.

His good indoor shoes were entirely wrong for this sort of spelunking, but Finn hadn't had time to fetch his wellies from the far side of the manor before sneaking out. His opportunities were rare these days, between his lessons and Mabel's overbearing eye.

The lighthouse winked in the distance through the gathering dusk.

Nearly to the shore, a few feet to the left, Finn found the gap in the enormous stones he was looking for. From his rucksack, he pulled out the handheld electric torch his mother had given him for his last birthday. He switched it on and slid carefully down into the cave.

The space wasn't big, but it did stretch nearly ten paces beyond Finn, ending just at the far reaches of the light from his torch. The water slipped in for a visit there and then swept back out to the open ocean, carrying its leagues of secrets with it.

When he'd first discovered this spot, nearly ten months ago in the early fall, Finn had slipped on a particularly briny patch of seaweed above and slid his way right down into the cave. It had been, in essence, an entry into another world. He'd had bruises for weeks, but they'd been worth the discovery.

This evening he made it down without injury. He crouched on the foam-speckled rock and pulled the rest of the goodies from his bag: the rolls, the books, a shiny apple, a thermos of soup.

"Seashell?" The voice came from where the rocks met the water.

"Seaweed," Finn said back with a grin. He turned the torch away from her face, but there was still just enough light to make her out, head bobbing in the water. Her hair glowed. Finn didn't think he knew the word to describe its color.

"I brought more today," he said, gesturing to the spread in front of him.

"More of what?"

"Food." She was silent. "Books." This won him the desired response: she laughed. She disappeared under the little lapping waves, a silver flash in her wake. When she reappeared, she placed her hands on the rocky ledge, coming as close to land as she dared.

"Thank you," she whispered. Finn could hear her clearly over all the sounds of the sea.

"Two more Christies," he said. Discovering that his new friend had a thirst for murder mysteries had been a bizarre thrill. Luckily, Finn's mother kept her bookshelves thoroughly stocked. He didn't think she'd miss these few. "This one takes place on a train," he said, pointing. "It's like a boat, but it runs on metal tracks on land. You can even sleep on them." Finn did love to talk about trains.

"I've seen a train," his companion said. "Down the coast, there's one that runs alongside the water." She tilted her head, considering the cover of the book that Finn was holding up to show her. "I'd like to ride one someday."

Finn lit up. "It's magnificent," he said. "You can sit and eat sweets and watch the world go by outside your window and play cards for hours." He added a rather daft thing, then: "Someday, I'll take you on one."

"Someday," she agreed, her voice dreamy. "Now what smells so good?"

Finn called her Seaweed, because the day he slid into the grotto and met her, she'd appeared like a beast from the depths, come to consume him. Once he'd regained his bearings and assessed the gash on his shin, the slimy green creature peering at him over the edge of the rock's lip had been far scarier than the fall. His scout's training made Finn feel a bit brave, however, so when the monster made no move towards him, he only squared his shoulders and said. "Hello. Would you like to see some shells I found?" His pockets were full of them.

So, Seaweed had peeled her camouflage off enough that he could see she was just a girl around his age — its own rather serious shock — and told him he couldn't *imagine* the incredible seashells she'd seen. She called him Seashell from then on, anyway. Sometimes she brought him specimens he had to believe had come from the very sea floor. They shone with their own strange light from within.

He'd only seen Seaweed once again last fall before the winter came on; he'd happened to have a book in his bag and discovered her immense fascination with them for the first time. The rocks were near impenetrable once the ice set in, and he worried about how she kept warm out there. As spring melted into summer, he'd slipped Mabel's tight lead and snuck more books and tasty morsels out to his new friend.

She always returned the books he brought her, if a little thicker from water and laden with tiny sea stars and sand dollar bookmarks. He couldn't return them to his mother's shelf in that condition, which rather thwarted his plan to swap them in and out a few at a time, so he hid them underneath his bed instead. It was starting to smell like the sea in there.

He made a bargain with the housekeeper, Eileen, that she could rest in his room whenever she wanted during the day if she didn't clean under his bed for a while. So far, the accord was holding.

The summer was hot, the sea was a respite, and Finn was distracted all day from his lessons by the pull of the tide. And Seaweed. He'd never had a friend like her before.

She'd started finding him all over the shore. When he was collecting sticks to build out a fort in the forested spot on the edge of the land, Seaweed had appeared from around a rocky outcropping and floated him several enormous, water-logged pieces of driftwood for his project. She could only come so near, but in his roughest clothes, Finn waded out to catch hold of them once they drifted close enough.

Once, while taking a long walk with some visiting great uncle at the gentleman's request, Finn had seen the silver flash amongst the waves gathering offshore that he knew — *knew* — was Seaweed. He stuck his tongue out in her direction while the man mused aloud about the terrible temperament of swans.

Another time, taking his lunch by the sea with Mabel knitting contentedly in her seat in front of him on the dock, Seaweed had started popping her head up, pulling faces behind Mable's back. Finn laughed uncontrollably as she disappeared before the poor woman could see what was so funny, only to reemerge on her other side time and time again. Understandably, Mabel was rather cross with him all evening.

She was good at finding Finn wherever he went, so long as it was along the sea. Finn learned that she loved Hercule Poirot but didn't so much care for Ms. Marple. He learned that her hair took on the color of the weather. He learned that she liked aged cheeses best of all the things he brought her to try, an opinion he wholeheartedly agreed with.

"I have *food*, Seashell," she'd said when he expressed concern he wasn't bringing her nearly enough. "I've a whole ocean of food. Delicacies you can't imagine. It's just that none of them taste quite like bread and cheese," she added with a little sniff. Finn, brave as he was, declined her offer to try raw sea urchin next time they met.

That day, Seaweed had asked him to bring her a book of French words next. She'd taken such a shine to Mr. Poirot that Finn felt an odd pang of what might have been jealousy. Could one be jealous of a character from a novel? Finn thought he would make a fine detective himself, though he didn't say this to Seaweed.

One day he'd solve a very famous crime, something that gripped the entire nation in its grisly clutches until he alone uncovered the final clue and revealed the perpetrator. (His gut had been right all along!) Then he would bring Seaweed the newspaper and show her the headline: *BOY DETECTIVE NEW HEAD OF SCOTLAND YARD.* No matter that he lived in Massachusetts. Seaweed would know that she had a friend even better than Hercule. Or at least as good as. Finn wasn't entirely confident he would've been able to sort out that Orient Express mess himself.

"I'm going to invent an underwater train," he told Seaweed one day. He was fishing off the dock, visible from the house. Mabel and Eileen were hanging the laundry out back on the veranda, but they would've had to come much closer to see his companion. She had streaks of sand in her hair, little green streamers dripping water onto her shoulders as she bobbed. Finn glanced at the silver flash in the water below her and away again.

Her eyes lit up at this suggestion, and she twirled around twice, giddy. "What a perfect idea," she said. "Imagine your people, looking out the window and coming face to face with a whale!" Her laugh sounded like a crashing wave. Finn would've recognized it on any shore.

"Sleeper cars with seafoam mattresses," he pitched. "Every drink will have bubbles in it. The seats will be made from enormous seashells."

"Less comfortable than you'd think," Seaweed countered. "You should see some of the interior decorating that goes on down here." She wrinkled her nose a little. "Tacky, if you ask me."

Finn couldn't begin to imagine.

As the cold rose again, Finn felt it creeping around his heart like a frost.

He hadn't had many friends before Seaweed. An eclectic, homebody mother and absent father made him a poor social mark. Now that he mainly took lessons at the house, he had few other children to play with, aside from Davie and Maxwell at Scouts meetings. His mother took visitors, many elegant, studious-looking men and women — sometimes also in a chair, like his mother was — who came and were kind to Finn, but they weren't his friends. Mabel and Eileen might've listened to him expound the intricacies of the newest diesel-powered locomotives, but they weren't exactly his friends, either.

Seaweed was his friend, though. So long as he could keep her reading. The pile under his bed was getting rather large, and his minders were growing more suspicious as the weather turned crisp. When Finn snuck off to the craggy shore, any door he opened let in a chill gasp of air, tattling on his escape. Still, he found Seaweed whenever he could.

"*Bonjour*," she greeted him. Her accent had gotten much better, once Finn had clumsily explained to her the little he knew of the language. He hadn't told her the French dictionary and workbook he brought her had been his own, so now he was without. She hadn't returned those to him yet. He didn't mind.

"*Coquillages*," she added, holding up a handful of seashells towards him in explanation. He knelt near her by the edge in the grotto and examined his gifts. In return, he'd brought her hot little hand pies, his mother's favorite. They'd been so fresh he burned two fingertips swiping them.

"*Merci*," he said, and when Seaweed smiled at him, he saw she was missing a tooth. They were the same, he thought, no matter what world they each went to sleep in.

"When are you going to take me on a train?" she asked as he left. She asked him this every time he left, now. The sun was already setting; he was sure once he climbed back up, he'd hear Mabel calling for him.

"Soon," he said, just as he did every time she asked. He meant it. He really meant it. Scout's honor.

"Finn," his mother said, tilting his face to hers.

Vera was shorter than him in her chair and had been for several years now, but he still felt her presence to be enormous. She was a busy woman, even though she rarely left home. She published work consistently under a pseudonym, which Finn couldn't understand — he wanted *everyone* to know her brilliant work was by her. His mother took visitors, edited manuscripts for friends, and wrote an unbelievable stream of outgoing correspondence. The manor had been specially fitted for her wheels to maneuver through years ago, and she lived more easily here than anywhere out in the world.

The way she sat by the window and looked at the sea made Finn wonder sometimes if she longed for more. He couldn't ask her such a thing, though.

"Finn," Vera said again, and he met her eyes. She was unusually serious. It was a rare thing to have his mother angry with him. He bit his lip and shifted his weight.

"Yes, Mother?"

"Would you care to tell me what on earth has happened to my books?"

Finn's eyes widened, darted behind his mother to the four inlaid bookshelves ringing her study. He thought he'd been doing a perfectly good job of rearranging things subtly every time he took a new volume, disguising the holes. He'd been fooling himself to think his mother wouldn't notice.

"I've, uh, borrowed — a few," he stammered. Vera only looked at him steadily. "To read," he added, as though that might help. She raised one fine eyebrow.

"And why, I might ask, are they turning up like this?"

Alas, his agreement with Eileen had apparently come to an abrupt end. He eyed the stiff, faintly green copy of *Little Women* he'd stashed under his bed months ago now. Even fully dried, it smelled pungently of the sea.

Finn met his mother's gaze again. She placed the book gently in her lap, like the grimy thing belonged with her. "Tell me, darling," she said. Finn looked out the window behind her at the rolling, gray tide breaking against the rocks. He wondered where Seaweed would ride out the advancing storm.

"I made a friend," he said.

That night, once all the lights were out except in Vera's study, she sat in her chair looking out the same window. It was dark, but she knew where the sea lay. Finn had fallen asleep on the sofa in her study hours before, but Mabel had at last come to fetch him for a bath and sleep in his own room. His room full of books from the sea.

Vera had noticed her shelves thinning for months; she was too keen not to. She would never punish her son for his hunger to read, even if she was curious about his secrecy.

She'd had no idea the strange, impossible tale he would tell her by way of explanation. He hardly seemed to believe it himself.

Vera's body ached. She'd been in the chair for too long without a break today. She finished the few fingers of whiskey she'd poured herself and wheeled towards her bathroom, her enormous copper tub nearly full. It was her favorite part of the house, aside from that window. She peeled off the layers of blankets she always wore carefully tucked around herself in her chair one by one, sighing in relief.

Beneath them, her tail looked dull, nearly lifeless. It was cool and clammy to the touch. Vera winced. She'd pushed it too far today. Her son's story had awoken a feral sort of longing in her that she usually held at arm's length: a beautiful, perished creature, wings spread and secured under glass.

With a great, heaving sigh, Vera hauled herself from the chair over the edge of the tub, water splashing gleefully on the floor. Decades, and she still hadn't figured out a smoother way in.

Under the water, her tail gleamed.

About the Author

Bridget grew up in the woods of the Pacific Northwest, and now spends her days navigating the wilds of Brooklyn. After a lifetime of reading and longing to write, she is publishing her first short story with Knight Writing Press and has a pair of novels currently in process. She is primarily concerned with eating as much sushi as possible, playing board games with pals, blasting music on winding country drives, consuming artfully arranged cheese platters, and her roommate's cat.

The Shrinking Island

by

Read Gallo

The Shrinking Island

Before the taming of magic, the island was shrinking. Some people said the cadassi, or as you might call them merfolk, were eating the shoreline. Fishers went missing, gnawed bones washed ashore shore and the coconut trees rotted where they stood.

Hunaisa did not care.

She picked up a dragon fruit and hurled it at the nearest palm tree.

Katango was a stupid vicious, stupid handsome, stupid waste of air and land, and Hunaisa was sorry she'd ever seen his face.

The dragon fruit slapped into the tree and rolled back to her feet.

Inviting her to dance at the prayer feast! She'd been caught off guard. She wasn't from a powerful family. She wasn't pretty. But she'd been flattered, and she'd stammered and flushed and accepted. Then he laughed.

Hunaisa picked up the dragon fruit again and threw it this time at a rock shaped like Katango's head.

All his stupid, vicious friends laughed at her.

The dragon fruit splattered on the rock, spiky pink skin splitting and juice spilling.

She'd lost her temper and made a fool of herself. She ought to have cried beautifully into her cousin's shoulder until someone chastised Katango for being unkind to a sensitive and lovely girl.

Hunaisa kicked half the dragon fruit along the path beside the bathing spring.

She ought to have kept her temper and smiled. "Oh, good. You were joking. I thought I would have to go through it and endure your stench." Then tossed her hair and walked away swiveling her hips.

The dragon fruit rolled into the water.

But no! She'd lost her temper and punched his stupid, handsome face. The chief, who was also Katango's uncle, had scolded her for causing trouble during a time of crisis. She'd been sent out of the village for the night, ashamed. If she hadn't been so angry, Hunaisa might have been afraid. Her mother told her to beg for mercy and stay in the safety of the village—that's what everyone did. But Hunaisa had been humiliated enough by Katango's family for one day, and she didn't care if she got eaten by fish-people or rotted like the coconut trees or washed out to sea because apparently even the land wasn't behaving like it was supposed to anymore.

She growled and sat by the spring. She'd come there by habit, since whenever she left the village with the other girls it was to come here to fetch fresh water and bathe. She'd sat next to a pile of lemon peels that everyone used to make their hair shine.

Grandma said it was important to drink when you'd been crying and Hunaisa had been crying with her anger all day. So, she picked up a handful of the rinds and swam out into the water.

No one would notice the shine of her hair if she disappeared. No one would care if she disappeared. Mother would probably be happy she never had to beg for her stupid, vicious, not-handsome daughter.

Hunaisa thought maybe she wouldn't go back to the village. She could live forever in the wilderness. Find a cave and be a mean-spirited magic-woman. She'd fish for herself and curse the town. More likely she's get eaten by the cadassi, but Grandma also said it's good to dream.

Hunaisa dreamed she'd got her own island as a mean-spirited magic-women and when the stupid, handsome boys glimpsed her from afar and she was so achingly beautiful that they would swim out to get closer to her. She dreamed that the vicious ones would drown or dash against the rocks.

Then she realized someone else in the water behind her.

"This counts as outside of the village, and I won't leave until the chief himself forces me too!" Hunaisa shouted without looking.

"What?" The other girl had a softer voice and the kind of mushy, big eyes that made a woman look like a child if she didn't glare. "Sorry!"

Hunaisa did not recognize the other girl, which meant the stranger had traveled quite far from her own home. Maybe the shrinking island was pushing the villages together and there would be a war, too. But a traveler might have a safe place to sleep at night, so Hunaisa softened her own face and smiled. "I said, hello, friend. I'm Hunaisa from Agana Springs. Who are you?"

The girl smiled and swam nearer in the purple-red water. "P…pleased to meet you. I'm Attau f-f-from Flower Lagoon."

Flower Lagoon. Hunaisa had never heard of it, but this stuttering girl keeping her distance couldn't be a threat. Her hair hung in a loose sheet, and it did not shine. "Are you far from home? Come here and I'll plaid your braids and make them shine."

"I am. I came with fishers, and I got lost." Attau swam nearer. Her way of swimming, without really using her arms, was as funny as her way of talking. "I do like how your hair shines."

Hunaisa flipped the braids over her hand, pleased with the silky smoothness. "It's the simplest thing. Lemon peels."

"Lemon." Attau repeated as if she'd never heard the word and nodded.

"Where have you been sleeping?" Hunaisa asked. "I'll share my food if you'll let me stay there with you. If it's safe. In the morning, I will take you to my village and our elders will help you get home."

Attau relaxed and smiled. She had a radiant smile, and her teeth were like pearls. "I— Thank you. So much!"

"Of course." Hunaisa crushed the lemon rinds in Attau's dark hair. Her hair was tangled but salt-softened between her fingers.

"I've been staying in the grotto just under there. I've been too afraid to go far from it. I don't know if the great fish will chase me again."

"Great fish?" Where was this girl from? "Like a shark or a whale?"

"Yes. Only more so. More teeth. More size." Attau flinched, embarrassed. "Sorry. I… I meant… The great fish is bigger than a whale and has more teeth than a shark. I've never seen anything like it."

"It's alright. I understand." Hunaisa took her time squeezing the lemon and raking it through her new friend's hair. There wasn't a noisy crowd of people around demanding their turn or gossiping about stupid boys. "I've never heard of the great fish."

A little fin brushed her leg as Attau spun around to face her. Hunaisa thought nothing of it. Fish were plentiful in the bathing spring.

"Your village isn't troubled by the great fish!" Attau's eyes brightened.

"My village has many troubles, but a fish isn't one of them." Hunaisa took the girl's shoulder and moved her back into position. Her skin was…unusually soft, almost spongey. "You must stay still, or I won't be able to get your braids straight."

Attau relaxed again and let Hunaisa play with her hair. "I'd like very much to see your village. The great fish crushed our stores of crabs and clams. It tore up our kelp farms. It even broke one of our pipes."

Hunaisa braided quietly and made noises as if she understood. But she knew by now, she wasn't braiding the average stranger's hair. Maybe all her dreaming delivered her into the hands of an actual magic-woman. She regretted dreaming. "The great fish sounds terrible."

"Well," Attau chuckled. "Not as terrible as the humans, though, right? Eating the tails off people and spitting out the rest to bob into town. My father—he's a guard—he thought one of the poor fellows was drunk and swam out to demand he answer his calls. He was shaking for days. They let him stay on the upper level because he got the gasps."

Kelp farms and pipes. Bobbing… Tails…

Hunaisa glanced down in the water, but in the evening light she could not see below the big billowing dress the girl wore. "What a terrible thing. I hope he will recover soon."

"Oh, it's not a real sickness. Just, you know…" Attau imitated breathless fear, like waking from a dream. Then smiled over her shoulder. "I'm sure such dignified people as you inland folk have a nicer word for it."

"Night terrors." Hunaisa answered confidently. Inland? She lived as close to the water as a human could. "My uncle had them for a time. He was gored by a winged piglet."

"A winged piglet? What a strange—" Attau's smile fell. Her gaze drifted into the water, too. She cleared her throat after a difficult swallow. "My dear new friend, Hunaisa, what kind of food will you bring for our dinner?"

Hunaisa dropped the girl's half-finished braid and reached for the sharpened bone tied to her hip. "Mangos and sweet bread. My friend baked it fresh today. How far will we walk to your shelter?"

Attau answered coldly. "We must swim there."

Both girls moved at the same time, splashing away from each other and drawing their weapons. Hunaisa darted to the shallower water and pointed her dagger. Attau with a roll of her purple-black tail curled into deeper water and pointed two evil-looking sticks lined with shark-teeth.

"What are you doing in our fresh-water pool, you lying fish-woman?" Hunaisa demanded.

"You're the liar. I didn't know monkeys could swim!"

"Are you poisoning our water?" Hunaisa gestured with the dagger threateningly.

"I wouldn't! And what did you do to my hair?" Attau tried to flick her hair into her face, because she didn't want to lower her tooth-sticks. "Were you going to cut it and use it in one of your twisted magic rituals?"

"Our twisted magic rituals? You fish-people are the ones who drown fishers and leave their bones gnawed on beaches."

"Well, your people harvest cadassi scales and turn them into beads."

"No. We don't! That's disgusting." Hunaisa grimaced, then realized. "Wait, humans also don't eat cadassi and leave half of them to bob in the water."

Attau narrowed her eyes, which looked quite fierce now. "We don't drown fishers. We spear and we cut off heads."

"So do we!" Hunaisa lifted her dagger threateningly.

"No. I meant..." Attau lowered her sticks. "We don't gnaw on human bones and leave them on beaches. We use bones in our building, but not human bones."

Hunaisa realized Attau was having trouble getting her meaning right again, but her tone had gentled. She was trying to be diplomatic.

Attau lifted one hand and touched her forehead with her index finger to indicate she was thinking. "I mean… We, cadassi, don't drown humans. Or anyone. Drowning is cruel. The worst way to die."

Hunaisa lowered her dagger. "We, humans, don't hunt the cadassi. We wouldn't leave half a person floating—like bitten in half? Like something is eating cadassi?"

"And humans, too!" Attau nodded. "If you have people missing."

Attau swam into deeper water and floated on her back. This gesture lifted her hips and showed her shark-teeth sticks sliding back into the belt across her belly. Her tail was longer than a person's legs and had the beautiful iridescence of an orca. "Let's talk again. You on the shore and me in the water. Weapons away."

"Agreed." Hunaisa climbed on shore. She sat on the rocky ledge, crossing her legs.

"Oh, wow," Attau said.

"What?" Hunaisa demanded.

Attau shook her head defensively. "I only… I've never seen a human's legs before. You're not really like a monkey at all."

Hunaisa supposed that was a compliment. "You're not really a fish, if you fear drowning."

Attau shrugged and flipped in the water, dampening her head, but not quite untangling her hair. When she surfaced, she said, "Let me tell you about the great fish."

Hunaisa leaned over the water. "Let's start with how a cadassi swam into this spring from the ocean."

At dawn, Hunaisa returned to her village exhausted and trembling. Would she ever stop trembling? She'd seen…the size of it…she couldn't believe what she'd seen. She had a duty to make the elders of Agana Springs believe in something she couldn't believe.

Katango leaned on top of the wall, as if he'd been there all night waiting to mock her. In another time, she might have let

her eyes linger on his bare chest and admire the reflection of the
pink sunlight on his brown skin, but today she wondered what
she'd ever seen in him. He looked mean-lipped and spoiled
when he sneered. "Oh, so you came back to beg?"

Hunaisa ignored him. She approached the main gate.

Katango walked along the top wall glaring at her through the
purple swelling of his blacked eye. "Your mother cried all night."

"If you have any good in you, you'll run to her now and tell
her I'm all right."

There was no good in him. "My uncle won't let you back in.
He says people who cause trouble in a time of crisis are the
worst kind of people."

"Then I'll look forward to your company beyond the walls in
a few days." Hunaisa did not rise to his bait, and it felt strange to
be so calm. Maybe it was because she had a higher purpose.
Maybe she was still in shock. All those teeth... Boulders and
sand tumbling into its huge throat.

Hunaisa reached the main gate. "Grandfather Pution."

Pution wasn't her grandfather by blood, but in a place as
small as Agana Springs, everyone was family. He nodded at her
through the slates of the gate and poked his actual
granddaughter in her side. The little girl—eight and plump—
woke up and blinked at him. "Run and tell Hunaisa's mother
that her daughter is safe."

The little girl turned her blinking towards Hunaisa, then
leaped to her feet and dashed off.

Pution offered her a loaf of sweet buns. "I cannot let you in
without the chief's say-so, and he's given very strict orders. But I
can share my bread."

Hunaisa reached through the gate and pulled off some buns.
Pution changed the tearing to give her more. "Thank you."

"Did you find safety?"

"No. I saw—"

What could she say?

*I went to the freshwater spring, mad as a goat. I met a cadassi. She
showed me the teeth marks in the rock, the new path to the sea from where
we women bathe.*

Then its shadow hid the moon and the redness of its eyes.

"I...I'm not ready to talk about it yet. When the chief gets here. I will."

"Eat and get your strength."

Hunaisa was so glad Pution was the guard this morning.

Katango jumped off the wall. "You're just causing more trouble. You'll tell any lie to get back into the village."

Hunaisa ignored him. Maybe the calm came from hunger. She ate Pution's gift. Maybe she was too scared to feel anger at such a small thing as Katango anymore.

"Pution," Katango didn't even have the courtesy to call the old man 'grandfather.' Yesterday, she might have thought it meant he was strong and commanding, but today it just seemed rude. "Make her tell what she saw. She's just trying to make trouble— If I were chief, I would have put her to death instead of—"

"Katango!" Pution's voice was stern as a falling rock. "Get your uncle."

The boy had the instinct to disobey, but the old man fixed him with such a cold-fish look that he ran.

Pution drank the broth he'd been boiling then offered some to Hunaisa. "He will never be chief with that attitude."

Hunaisa agreed. "No. He says...chief-like things, but he doesn't mean them, I think."

"He's a self-important ass, who never thinks of anyone besides himself, and parrots whatever wisdom manages to sneak between his ears."

Hunaisa smiled and sipped the broth. "Grandfather, you've been a fisher your whole life. Have you ever met a cadassi?"

The old man rubbed his chin. "It's unlucky to talk about the cadassi, but I have. Many times. When you sail into their water, they greet you with spears and shrill screams. Some people think it's rude, but I've also guarded this gate, and I can't imagine how I would react to people flying overhead with nets and spears."

"I've heard them singing on the rocks." Hunaisa said carefully. "They seem intelligent."

"Oh, no doubt." The old man paused—superstition or wisdom. "One saved a young man I knew from drowning. They've been known to do that, you know."

"Drowning is cruel. They think it's the worst way to die," Hunaisa said quietly.

Pution nodded understanding.

Katango, reliably, brought half the village along with his uncle. Hunaisa's mother brought the other half, crying now with happiness as she tried to hug her daughter through the wooden slats of the gate.

"Uncle," Katango talked endlessly. "She only wants to cause a fuss."

Hunaisa realized, for the first time, something about her frightened Katango. Perhaps it was the way she spoke over him without fear, looking directly at the chief. "He's not wrong, Chief. There's a great deal going wrong, and if I tell you what I saw it will cause a fuss."

Katango began, "Inciting panic—"

The chief lifted his hand and even his nephew fell silent. "No one will interrupt you, Hunaisa. Tell us what you saw last night."

Hunaisa had to catch her breath. She realized she had not been sent out of the village by accident. The chief had hoped she would have news. A strange clear-headed calmness floated through her, and Hunaisa said exactly what she'd planned. "When I left you all yesterday, I walked to the bathing pool, and I saw there was a tide."

The clever people looked from one to another. The fresh-water springs should not have tides.

"I dropped in some rinds, and I watched where the current pulled them and found a new tunnel under the water. There were coconut tree roots, bite marks, signs of something burrowing. I went as far as I dared and let the lemons go, then I walked to the shore to see where they washed up."

Attau had done all the swimming, and she'd been able to tell Hunaisa exactly what shore to look for.

"The bay that has been getting deeper and darker. There are teeth marks on those rocks." Hunaisa was no longer lying. "That's where I saw…"

She still didn't believe what she'd seen. How could she expect these people to believe?

"Saw what?" the Chief asked.

"A great thing in the water. When it lifted its head, it blotted out the moonlight."

Katango made a face and was about to say something, but the chief spoke first. "What else did you see? Did it burrow?"

"I didn't see that," Hunaisa confessed. "But I have no doubt it would. I lured it to North beach by banging together coconuts and shouting. I wanted to get it away from the bathing pool before it fully broke through."

And so Attau could escape to the open sea, so the cadassi with the stutter could have this same conversation with her tribe.

"On North Beach, it picked up the boulder and crushed it into pebbles and swallowed it."

Even the not-so-clever people gasped and understood that. The boulder at North beach was unmovable. Even the tides broke around it.

"You can walk to North Beach and see for yourselves if you don't believe me. I think the beast prefers to eat softer things, like humans and cadassi. I think if left to its own devices it will bite the island to pieces."

When it was clear Hunaisa had finished—and this is the first time she was aware of how many were standing silently listening to her—there was an uproar. She had expected people not to believe her. To stalk as one to the north beach. Instead, people cried, "It's the god of the sea. It wants a sacrifice," and "We're doomed!" and "How can we fight a monster large enough to swallow a boulder whole?"

Katango's voice boomed over the others, "We must drive it away and turn it on the cadassi."

Hunaisa scoffed. "And what's to stop it from turning around once it wreaks havoc among them?"

"Well, then what would you do?" Katango accused. "Let it eat the whole country?"

Hunaisa snorted in answer.

The chief asked, less an accusation and more earnest. "Hunaisa, how would you deal with the monster?"

She shifted uncomfortably. They were supposed to go to the beach. At the beach, if the cadassi people listened to a young girl trapped in a bathing pool and rescued by a human, her village would have been greeted by a band of cadassi warriors ready to fight the monster with them.

"I would…" Hunaisa looked at her mother for strength. "I would trap it inland."

"And how do you plan to do that? It won't exactly fit in a fish trap." Katango demanded.

When Hunaisa had no answer, the chief frowned and shook his head. "We will hunt it in the open waters, as we do the man-eating sharks."

"I don't think you understand the size of it," Hunaisa protested. "Or its speed. Even the cadassi can't kill it in the water. We must trap it and—"

"How do you know the cadassi can't kill it in the water?" Katango demanded.

"Because…" Hunaisa had no answer. "Well, if they could, they would have."

Katango grinned and sprang his trap. "You've been talking to the fish-people."

Hunaisa crossed her arms and glared. "Katango, we have a man-eating monster large enough to bite through—"

"For all we know the cadassi brought the giant fish here and are using this troublemaker to help them. Why haven't our fishermen encountered this thing if it's big as she says?"

"They have," Hunaisa replied. "And they haven't survived."

It was Katango's turn to stagger for words.

The chief spoke for them both. "If it does exist, we must kill it in open water. This will preserve our freshwater pool and show our might at sea."

By midmorning, every boat in the village was out on the water, filled with the strongest and bravest warriors on the island.

By noon, every boat in the village had been reduced to splinters.

Hunaisa stood on the shore and watched the destruction besides a handful of villagers, including her mother and Pution. The monster—which looked like a giant eel—crashed amid the driftwood that used to be boats. The spears and nets were not fast enough. The monster seemed like oil, like water itself and no one—not even Katango—managed to spear it. And each miss meant the monster had the time to attack.

So many people were in the water, then in the monster's teeth. It reared its head as it fed, and its flat teeth were streaked with blood.

The villagers on shore shouted in anguish. They called the names of fishers and warriors stranded in the water. They begged, "Swim to shore!" and "Hurry!" They shouted to the sun and the sea to have mercy.

The monster heard the people on shore and with a shrill scream, charged toward the villagers.

"Get back from the sand," Hunaisa fled toward the trees. She'd found out last night, just how fast the monster was, how nimble it was digging through the sand, how effortlessly it snatched chunks of the island and swallowed the shore.

The villagers followed her to the trees and the monster followed them, throwing its slender body out of the water. The sand flew like raindrops, and the snake-body growled and snapped at the fleeing villagers.

"Swim to shore and surround it!" shouted the chief from the water.

"Don't run to the village or you will draw it there," shouted Hunaisa. "Get onto tall rocks and keep its attention so they can flee the water."

"Help! Help!" howled Katango thrashing in the water.

Hunaisa scrambled to the high cliff where she'd spent most of the night. From that height, she clapped coconuts together and sang—a silly child's song—and the monster wriggled after her with tiny, sightless eyes and a million teeth. But as long as she sang and clanged coconuts it wasn't in the water eating her villagers.

Her mother was the first to join her in clapping coconuts and singing. Then Pution. Then all the children of the village who were with them. It was a strange thing to see—dozens of elders and children singing and smacking sticks and coconuts and rocks to make noise while a huge man-eater flailed below them.

The warriors grew quiet in the water, except for the splashes of their swimming.

Hunaisa wondered what happened to Attau. Perhaps, she'd been eaten. Perhaps, the cadassi were bad after all. Unreliable at least. Or perhaps Attau had merely not been very convincing. Hunaisa couldn't hold it against her.

Then the warriors in the water started to cry out. White foam streaked around them as they swam. No. Not swimming. Their arms flailed and their torsos were out of the water.

Were they drowning?

"Hunaisa!" Attau called from the water. "We are here!"

Then Hunaisa saw the cadassi in the water. Long lean bodies carrying the warriors toward the shore. Quick as minnows and leaping from the water now and then to call to each other. "Bring the humans to shore!" and "Keep their heads out of the water!"

Katango resisted, and it took two cadassi to hold him above the water as they sped toward the shore.

The monster heard the thrashing and with a mouthful of cliff, it turned and slithered back toward the water.

"No! Here! Eat us!" Hunaisa shouted and threw her coconut at the beast.

Pution opened his pack and tossed bread and fruits at the monster's open maw. "Eat here!"

The monster snapped at the coconut and the bread and chewed at the rocky cliff to get closer.

The warriors came from the water, startled to be alive, surprised when the cadassi handed back their spears and pointed at the monster. Hunaisa stomped and sang as loud as she could when the chief took up his spear. She saw the cadassi in the water, sleek black hair and huge dark eyes bobbing in the surf waiting to see if the monster could be killed on land. Attau's hair was still braided, and it floated in the ocean.

When the humans threw their spears, they hit the monster's slippery sludgy body. Its blood spouted purplish black then red as the blood washed away the sludge covering its skin. But only the first few spears hit, then the monster darted and twisted and writhed on the sand, avoiding every other hit and roaring at the warriors. Most escaped to the trees, but a few unlucky ones were caught in its jaws and bit clean in half, then swallowed whole.

The cadassi had their own spears and daggers and waited in chilling silence for the monster to return to the water. But just like on land, only a few were fast enough to surprise the monstrous creature, before it dove deep into the water and escaped.

The island shook and a hill rose in the beach as the beast ate its way through the sand and into the forest. Coconut trees shivered and collapsed into the empty tunnel.

"It eats through the roots," Hunaisa said. "That's what rots them."

Attau called from below. "Be careful on your way home, my friend. There will be new rivers when the tide comes."

The chief stood with his spear in his hand, purposefully posing in the shallow water. "The island will become a swamp and all our trees and farms will be eaten from underneath if we cannot find a way to kill this thing."

One of the cadassi, two shark-tooth daggers in her hand and many necklaces of kelp and fishbones in her wild hair, curled her tail underneath her and rose next to him in the surf. "If we cannot find a way to kill the thing, it will eat everything solid, and both our people will drown and starve."

"H-h-hun—my friend," Attau gestured for Hunaisa. "Tell them we have a plan."

"We do?" Hunaisa didn't know about any plan.

"Just get the leaders to l-l-listen to me—to you—and I'll explain."

Hunaisa stoked her newly shorn scalp, feeling the prickles of tiny hair under her hand. Her head felt so light, and yet haunted by the ghosts of her braids. Strange to be as bald as the old men.

Her cousin actually cried, as she tied her newly chopped braids together, like a tiny ladder.

Katango, who's face seemed too round without his flowing locks, bent over in front of his uncle and held his knees while he panted. "The monster is...south side of the island...Pution's group."

The chief nodded. He had been the first to cut his braids. "It won't be long now."

Katango glanced at Hunaisa, withholding a glare but only just. "The pork reserve is nearly gone."

This was more important the pork reserve and Katango knew it. Just as long as the monster was away from the cadassi, away from this beach, and could be lured...

The best weaver in Agana Spring shouted. "Everyone, tie up your edge. The net is finished."

It was a quick and messy net, but still the work of several dozen masters working at breakneck speed. The crisscrossing mass of black and brown hair spanned the entire length of the beach and swept out into the surf, where the cadassi, similarly newly shorn, tied the last edges of their part of the net.

Attau crawled in the shallows and Hunaisa wandered over toward her.

Hunaisa said, "It is on the south side. Will your people have enough time to get to the spring?"

Attau nodded. "Yes. Will your people be able to lure it?"

Hunaisa glanced over to Katango who was still getting his breath. "Go tell Pution it's time."

He glared at her, still doubled over and panting. But he turned and ran again.

Hunaisa said to Attau. "We'll wait for your signal."

The cadassi shivered with the responsibility. "I'll be on the bitten rock when we are ready."

Attau slipped away into the surf. Then the net disappeared into the waters.

The chief lifted his spear. Then the warriors disappeared into the forests.

The rest of the village, the weak ones, the elderly, the children, they looked to Hunaisa. She looked at the water and at the bite marks in the cliff.

The waves danced both steady and ever-changing, uninterested in the people watching above or the ones traveling below. There wasn't a single splash to indicate that the cadassi were setting a trap. Not a wave out of place to show they were not going back on their word and fleeing into the deeper ocean.

Not until—and it felt like hours later—Attau clambered awkwardly out of the water and crawled on top of the bitten rock. Hunaisa had stood on that rock last night when the tide was low and watched as the bay grew deeper and deeper as something huge ate its way to the freshwater pool where a little cadassi girl was trapped.

Attau waved both her arms and her tail.

Hunaisa waved back. "Alright, everyone. Start singing."

This was the night the village had planned to have their prayer dance. The whole village would have been singing at the center of Agana Springs. They might have accidentally lured the great fish directly underneath their feet. It would have swallowed every single person, except maybe one angry little girl who had punched the chief's nephew.

Now the village followed her away from the shore and toward the springs, maintaining their song, even when the sandy earth shook under their feet as something huge moved below them. When she reached the springs, Hunaisa saw the warriors standing perfectly still at the edges, weapons drawn. She kicked a fallen coconut into the spring where it splashed and floated out to the center. She could not hear the lap of the water over the singing of the village.

Katango stood beside the chief in the shadows, spear high. Pution and his group stood with the last of the reserved meat—probably the last meat left in the village—waiting to see if they needed to feed the creature again.

Then the still pool churned and frothed. Clay and bubbles and snail shells bobbed to the surface. Some people wavered in their singing, but the rest of the village made up for it.

The singing turned to a scream when the great fish came. A stream of sleek black sludge and a snarl of shadow finally broke into the pool and bit at the shore. The villagers barely escaped.

For a moment, Hunaisa's heart fell. Seeing the thing rise in her bathing pool, that huge head snatching at the coconut trees and sand, she knew they would fail. Her friend's plan had failed. Her allies were too weak. Nothing could defeat the bottomless appetite of this giant worm. She'd merely convinced the village to sacrifice themselves to this hungry sea-god. Cutting off their hair was just the first step to making them easier to digest.

Katango hoisted the spear on his shoulder, and she shouted. "Not yet!"

If they attacked now…if a stray spear made the beast turn back the way it came…the cadassi would be trapped in the underwater tunnel with that thing charging jaws first at them…

Katango looked at her, and held his spear.

With a bright splash, the first cadassi came through. It was Attau, and she carried her part of the net in both hands and swam fast toward the shore. The monster darted for her and Attau nimbly dodged by exploding out of the water and landing on the other side of the beast's snapping jaws.

Hunaisa thought she heard her friend laugh as she narrowly avoided death, but maybe it was the sound of a dozen other cadassi breaking the surface. Each carrying their part of the net. Each weaving and tangling the dark strands of hair over, and under, and around the thrashing beast.

"Now!" Hunaisa commanded when the last of the cadassi had splashed back into the pool.

A dozen spears flew, then a dozen more from the water.

The monster wailed and thrashed. It turned to escape, to writhe away from the spears, but the net twisted and trapped it more. But even with its tail in a knotted loop, it tried to feed.

When Hunaisa rushed into the water to grab the net, Katango joined her and so did the rest. The warriors reclaimed their spears and stabbed again. The rest grabbed the net and pulled it tighter.

The cadassi did the same, attacking with their shark-tooth sticks or wriggling out of the water with the nets alongside the humans.

The spring filled with sickly black bile and then bright red blood. The monster bit through the trunk of a coconut tree and broke bits of the net, but it could not escape.

It was dying. The plan was working.

The monster fixed its shiny eyes on Hunaisa and drew back its sharp rows of tiny teeth. Too late, Hunaisa realized the beast was about to strike and there was no way for her to escape its jaws.

Something black and sleek flashed out of the water, flying toward the monster's face. Attau's dagger landed in the monster's eye, and she grabbed the fin atop its head and swung her body and tail onto the top of the beast.

Forgetting Hunaisa, the beast railed and thrashed, but it could not buck the cadassi girl from its head. Attau drove her dagger deeper into the burst eye and into the brain and the beast shrieked, twitched, and then fell in a roil of bloody foam and black sludge.

Attau fell on the land, flopping in a most undignified way to get back to the filthy water. Hunaisa went over to help her, and Attau grinned up at her, teeth pearly in spite of her blood-streaked face.

"We should cook it. Your people should bring bread."

Hunaisa smiled back and helped Attau get back into the water. "That's the second-best plan you've had today."

About the Author

Read Gallo, writer and artist, hails from the most magical place in the world: New Jersey! A former pirate, mail-carrier, and tour guide, Read currently works as an administrator for a summer camp that protects, trains, and teaches children to be heroes. When not tending the trolls, herding the hydras, or polishing the pegasus, Read likes to create watercolor paintings and write stories about myths, legends, and fairytales. You can see the results at readgallo.com.

Behind the Jumble

by

Nick Clements

Behind the Jumble

Do you know what fear sounds like? How about pain? Do you know the sound of pain? Because I do. And it's a strange sound, it is. An eerie sound. Haunting. It's a sound that sticks in your chest, digging in, like a knife carving through bone. And it's a sound that I most likely won't never forget. Not in this life anyway.

We got the call just before eleven-thirty in the P.M. It was a Tuesday night I believe, early October, a hard wind pushing through, thin needles of rain spitting on down. I was riding shotgun, Officer Davis in the driver's side. We'd go out like this some nights. On most I'd ride solo, but not that night. That night I was with my friend, Officer Rick Davis. It would be the last time that I saw him.

The call relayed that there'd been complaints about some kids gone down to the beach by the harbor, had lit up a bonfire and were drinking and causing a ruckus as it were. It was standard fare for a Tuesday night. We were reluctant, this sort not being the most exciting, but we had to do a beach sweep at midnight anyway, so we figured we'd just start on that early, and so we headed on down there.

We were quiet in the truck, almost solemn. Rick's wife, Charlene, had been sick and recently passed. What she had inside her had been spreading for a while. Rick, by her side the whole lot of it, long days, long nights, suffered together through that painful time. I'd come and visit on occasion but dare not go in that there room. Couldn't bring myself to see 'em both like that. I'd wait in the hall, hat in hand, head down, listening to the moans, the cries and labored breaths. To Rick's muffled sobs.

I could tell Rick's mind was still there, as it had been those days, stuck back there with her sickness, her passing, ensnared in it. He'd taken some time off after, but not much. For men like Rick Davis, they need to work, because work for some men like Rick Davis, is sometimes the only way of escape. But what she had, and what they went through, I'm not sure if there was any way of escaping that.

Rick kept his steady pace ahead, clutching the steering wheel, his slicked red hair parted to the side, small strands whisking up from the breeze coming in from the cracked window. He could see me looking at him, wondering what was going on inside that head of his. That I could tell. Could see it in his cold stare. I hoped he knew I understood, or at least was trying anyway. We said nothing and kept driving along.

When we arrived at the beach, the rain had stopped, a shifting wind taking its place. A cold wind. It seemed that we had missed all the excitement. The beach was barren and desolate, absent of life, of youthful consumption. They must have caught word that we were on our way and fled the scene. We headed on down anyway, making our sweep.

We could see the remains of the bonfire in the distance; smoldering black logs held in the light of the moon, the smell of charcoaled wood thick in the air. We rumbled on down in the truck, the waves a hiss in the distance, moaning malignant, the ocean itself crying an exhortation that we both ignored. This was just a Tuesday after all, another day on the job, another sweep of the beach, a simple mundane shift to add to the rest. If only we had heeded the cries of the sea, we may have turned back, and things would be different. But that's not how it worked out. As rarely does.

As we were combing the beach, bored and unfulfilled as it were, left free of strife, something down the way caught Rick's eye. He leaned forward over the steering wheel, bottom lip curled. "The heck is that?" he whispered.

At the time I wasn't exactly sure what he was referring to, whatever it was lost to me, but Rick was sure of it alright, because he slammed that truck in gear and went speeding off toward the ocean line, toward whatever it was he thought he saw.

"Now hold on a sec now, Rick," I said.

But he didn't hear me, or didn't want to anyway, because he just kept on speeding along.

We got to the beachfront, and Rick slammed on the brakes and hopped out of the truck, quick-like, running on towards them foaming waves, his hand at his side clutching the butt of his service revolver. I was panicked a bit, not understanding the situation unfolding, fumbling with the door handle before I, too, hopped out and followed close behind.

When I got to him, he was just standing there, looking out at the ocean, as if he could see something, as if he knew what's out there. I turned to him confused. There was something in his eye, the way he looked out there. It was a look I recognized but couldn't quite put my finger on. But I could have sworn I'd seen it before, could have sworn it was the same look he had when he first heard the news about Charlene.

"What's going on there, Rick?" I asked.

He didn't respond.

"Rick!" I snapped.

He faced me, slow, cheeks drained of color. And he didn't say nothing, just held that insipid look back on me.

"What is it?" I asked quietly.

"You hear that?" he replied, the words drawn out.

"What?"

"I don't know."

"The fuck now?"

And he said no more.

I looked out at the spot he was staring, but I didn't see a thing. There just weren't nothing out there. I returned to Rick. His hand had dropped from the butt of his gun. "You okay?" I asked.

He gave me a slight nod of the head.

"What'd you see out there, buddy?"

He shrugged.

I turned back to the twisting sea, the taste of salt on my lips, the smell of brine suspended in the mist. "Well alright then," I said.

He brought his attention away from the ocean line, blowing hard through cupped hands around his mouth, his shoulders hunched in.

"What's going on?" I asked.

Rick brought his hands down to his sides. "I don't know," he replied in a whisper. "You ever get the feeling that something just ain't right with this place?"

"You mean this town?"

"No."

Now, I wasn't sure what Rick meant by that, but I stood by him. He was real shook by what he saw, or what he thought he saw anyway, that was clear, and I needed him to know that I was there and that whatever was ailing him, I'd be there to see it through no matter, as always. I felt I had to be that way, as if it were my duty or something. He'd been real bad off those last few months, Charlene's sickness and death taking its toll. He just wasn't the same Ol' Rick Davis I once knew. Something was off, something that I just couldn't quite figure.

I'd come to find out what that was later on, but for the time, I simply reserved to be there for him, and reassure him that I always would. But I'm all thumbs when it comes to matters such as those, just as I had been through the rough times he was going through. I did my best though, whatever that entailed.

"You wanna continue on down then?" I asked.

He was still in that daze, like a man who's been shot, now cradling his hands together, almost coy in his hunched stance. Then he brought those eyes back on me, glossy, laced with fear. Or something like fear anyway. "Yeah," he said quietly, "sure thing."

"Alright then."

We moved back to the truck. That's when I stopped, dead in my tracks, sand swallowing up my boots. Because I caught a glimpse of the sea in my peripheral, and I saw something out there, a figure of sorts behind the tumble of waves. I turned and looked closer. My eyes narrowed, adjusting. Then I saw it, no mistakin' *that*. Because there, shifting and bobbing in that there ocean, was a woman, topless and smiling wide.

I took a step forward to get a better look. The girl was naked from the waist up, wet hair draped on her shoulders, darkened from the sea, a strand of kelp slapped across her chest like a leach. She kept that stare on me with that bright face and stretched smile, gently bobbing up and down from the heaves of the ocean. Then she raised her arm and waved.

"Shoot," I said, "that's what's got you so shook, Rick?"

"No," he replied flatly.

"No what?"

"That ain't right, Lyle."

"What ain't right?"

"That girl there."

"Shoot, Rick, it's just a naked drunkard. Pay it no mind."

"No, Lyle."

"No what?"

"No."

Now Rick's behavior was curious alright, but I still had to do my job, with or without his sanction, if you follow. So, I grabbed my flashlight and shone it out there on the girl. "Hey there now, hon," I shouted. "Come on out there now."

Rick moved closer in front of me, his steps slow and timid, hand resting back on his sidearm.

"Go easy, Rick," I said. But he didn't hear me, or simply didn't listen, because he just kept inching forward.

I brought my attention back to the sea, the girl caught in the beam of my flashlight, one arm raised to shield her eyes. Then she looked back at me, dead in the eye she did, sharp yellow in the pupils, red lined on the sides. I'd seen that clearly from the shine of light. "The what?" I said. Then she dropped out of sight, sunk back into the darkened waters.

I moved the flashlight from the ocean and brought it back on Rick. His hand was shaking, there at his side, his body stiff. "You see them eyes?" I said. But he didn't say nothing back.

Then the radio squawked from the truck, and I snapped to and moved on over to it, poking my head through the cab to grab the C.B. It was a domestic dispute call if I'm not mistaken. Some others took it up. I placed the C.B. back in its holster and climbed out from the truck, bringing my glance back to where I last saw the naked girl. But there was nothing out there, just the tide turning. I took a look around, and Rick was lost to my sight as well.

"Gosh damn it, man," I said to myself as I began trudging down the beach in search of my partner.

I walked down to the little jetty on the right, the harbor at my back. I brought my hand up above my brow, as if this gesture would help me see through the darkness. I still didn't see nothing. I stood there for a while, searching, the spit from the sea smacking my face, a smell of farts and rot from the runoff choking the air. I pinched my nose and held down the sick, then brought my head back up, panning the beachfront.

"Rick!" I called. But nothing responded besides the rumble of waves and the low howl of wind. "Fuck, man, where'd you run off to now?"

I kept moving down the beach, past the jetty, the harbor shrinking behind. Then I slowed my pace as I saw something creeping from behind a dune of sand. At first, I thought it was just a mound of tangled up seaweed, but the seaweed was moving slightly, almost gentle like. I clipped the snap on my holster, hand slowly wrapping around the handle of my revolver as I proceeded on forward with caution.

Then I heard it.

It was a foreign sound; something strange and piercing. But I wasn't sure what it was, so I kept moving along. Then I heard something else, and I stopped right there. Because I realized what I heard that time. I reared my neck up past the sand dune, trying to make out that blackened mound. Then I'd seen what it was, and a sharp tingle rushed down my spine and into my ass.

It was my partner, my friend, Officer Rick Davis, lying on his back, a small, garbled moan emanating from his mouth as something shadowed lay hunched over him, digging into his torso.

"Officer Davis!" I cried. "You okay?"

He spat out that low moan again, muted against the crash of waves. "Uuunnng."

I brought my voice to a quiet hush. "Officer Davis?"

I kept heading toward him, his flaccid body inching back and forth, not moving per-se, just lightly jutting there in the sand. Then as I got to a few feet from him, I seen that shadow on top of him, seen it clearly. It was the naked girl from earlier, digging her head into Rick's torso, thrashing about his stomach with nary a care that I was coming right up on her.

I pulled my revolver from its holster and raised it up, pointed at the girl. "Hey there, hon, stop right there and bring them hands up where I can see 'em!" I hollered.

She popped up, face covered in blood, and snot, them yellow eyes darker somehow; bright orange and red like a mango sunset. And she just simply stared back at me with that silent content, me standing not ten feet away, frozen stiff and petrified.

Then she let out a hiss, a high-pitched sound, almost deafening to the ear. And this time I recognized it, knew exactly what it was, sure as Hell. And as the sound rang out in that whispered screeching echo, she started moving her torso, slowly wiggling back and forth like a serpent in a trance. Then she brought herself upright from behind Rick, and I could see the rest of her. I was shocked and horrified I was, got damned bewildered as it were, because I didn't know what I was looking at. Because what I was looking at didn't make a lick of sense.

The rest of her body wasn't no body I'd seen before; caught in the light from the white of the turning waves, an abundance of scales ran down her torso, starting up from her belly on down, sparkling there, dark green and black, menacing in its foreign design. And them scales seemed to grow somehow, wide and thick they were, moving on down to where her legs should have been, but there weren't no legs there. Nope, instead of where them legs should have been, there was instead a big ol' fat tail flopping there behind her.

My body was stiff as stone it was, no movement, not even a breath of air. And I just stood there, holding that revolver on her, whatever she was. Then she let out that sound again, and I could feel my legs begin to give, knees buckling. And suddenly I was somehow tempted to move closer, to be with her, hold her. I didn't know what was going on, and I didn't like it, but at that moment, all I wanted was nothing less than to be with that beautiful, strange creature hovering above my mutilated friend.

My mouth ran dry. "Now hold on a sec," I managed through my cracked throat. But that was all I could muster.

She brought her attention away from me, bored as it were, and continued on with her meal that once went by the name Officer Rick Davis, and there was nothing I could do; nothing but watch this horrid creature devour my friend. I felt the piss run down my leg. Then Rick stopped moaning.

The thing ceased its thrashing, head raised up from behind Rick's limp body, that there tail flapping up and about, specks of sand sprinkled behind. Then that too stopped, and the thing moved low and flat, elbows arched akimbo, and its jaw, like, *fell* as it were, plopping down to the sand before it snatched onto Rick bellow his belly, on his buckle like. Then it began whipping its head back and forth viciously, and started crawling back to the ocean, Rick snagged in its mouth where it slunk down, back into the crashing waves. And it, along with Officer Rick Davis, vanished into the sea.

Once it was gone, I still couldn't move; revolver raised, pants wet and reeking of piss. I stood there for quite a while I did, just listening to the gentle breeze and them rolling waves, pondering it all. I thought about that strange creature, that sound it had made. I had heard that there sound before, I did, right before Charlene died in fact. It's something you don't forget.

And I thought about Charlene. And her sickness, her death, that look stuck in poor Rick's eyes. I just couldn't shake that look, and to this day I still can't. Because I realize now what that look was. It was the same one he done gave me in the truck on our way to the harbor, the same one on that godforsaken beach. The look I'd seen those last few days of his life. It was a look as if to suggest he was done. Done with the sickness and the sadness and the fear, the death; done with it all I 'spose. And he was ready for it, it seemed, ready for that thing take him. I could see it in his eye and could hear that in that last moan he gave with a defeated push. It was all over him alright. He wore it like new skin. And, although I missed my friend, I was happy for him, in a way. He was finally relinquished from it all, from the pain and fear of this place. From the sickness.

After that, I never did partner up again, spending the rest of my days behind a desk as it were. I just couldn't stomach it no more I 'spose. They never did find out what happened to Ol' Rick Davis; his death remains an open case to this day. They asked me what had happened. I explained the best I could that he simply left this place. Now the only ones who know what truly happened out there on that fateful night are just me and the sea, and the creatures it holds.

And I couldn't set not one foot back in an ocean again after that night neither, not even a toe in the sand. Just couldn't do it, couldn't bring myself to. For I know what those haunting waves truly hold, know the sickness of it, the fear and the death that lurks behind the muted cries of the sea. And, well, I just couldn't stomach it no more. Couldn't stomach the strangeness of this world.

What was it that Rick had said? 'You ever get the feeling that something just ain't right in this place?'

Yeah, my friend, I get that feeling all the time.

About the Author

Nick Clements is an American writer whose short fiction has appeared in *Center Street Press*, *Samjoko Magazine*, *Pulp Cult*, and more. He currently resides in the Pacific Northwest.

Who Wants to Live Forever?

by

Brian MacDonald

Who Wants to Live Forever?

Rory just wanted an ice cream cone. Nothing much. Just one scoop of something sweet on a crunchy waffle cone. It was a hot day in July, and her tee-shirt was sticking to her. A drippy little ice cream would have been perfect.

Francis was absolutely certain that a banana split was in order. Chocolate, vanilla, and strawberry ice cream. Pineapple and strawberry sauces. Hot fudge. Whip cream. Nuts. A cherry on top. And the best one he knew was that Banana Bucket up in York, Maine by the lighthouse. It had six scoops and they were huge!

So, two hours later, after bombing up from Somerville in their old, beat-to-hell beast of a chevy with no air conditioning and waiting in line for what felt like an eternity, Rory held the fabled Banana Bucket in her hands.

It was huge.

She was pretty sure that a small family could feast off of it.

Francis could polish it off in one sitting. By himself, if Rory let him. She knew she would have to be strategic with her spoon. There was a spot at the zenith of the sundae where the chocolate, strawberry, and vanilla touched, covered in whipped cream and fudge. That was where she would start. Hopefully, she'd get a couple of spoonfuls before he wolfed down the whole damn thing.

Now, where the hell was he?

Rory turned, peering through the swath of ice cream lovers behind her in line. At her five-foot-two height, it was hard for her to see too far over and through them. That said, her six-foot-five husband tended to stick out from the crowd. He should have been easy to find. Nothing.

Rory stepped out of the line and wandered around, scanning the area. Did he go looking for somewhere to sit? No. The benches were all full of families with sticky kids in various stages of finishing off cups and cones.

She finally found Francis lumbering up the gravel driveway to the lighthouse. Where was he going now? Was he looking for a romantic spot to sit and eat? That would be nice and all, but it would have helped if he'd told her. If she hadn't spotted him, she'd have been walking around with a melting bucket of ice cream for who knows how long. Rory jogged to catch up with him as he continued his ascent.

"Hiya love. The banana bucket is ready for the eating. You have a dining spot in mind for us?" Rory matched pace with Francis, her feet crunching the stones along with him.

"Hmm?" Francis tilted his head absentmindedly to her. "Oh. Hey, honey. Do you hear that sound?"

"What sound?" Rory didn't hear anything unusual. Maybe the crash of the waves on the shore? The tide was coming in and appeared to be getting rough on the nearby rocks.

"The singing. It's beautiful."

"Singing? What singing?" Rory followed her husband until he turned the corner behind the lighthouse. And there, no more than a hundred feet away was a mermaid lying on the farthest rock outcropping. She was doing her best sexy photoshoot pose, waves crashing behind her lush, bright red hair as she leaned her heaving chest upward to sing.

"Oh. Wow. She's singing to me now, honey." Francis wandered closer to her, his face lit up with a stupid puppy dog smile. "She wants to go swimming." He stopped to hop on one foot to pull off a sneaker.

"Wait. Hold on to this." Rory thrust the banana bucket in his arms, right on top of the sneaker he'd gotten off. Francis almost fell over from his one-foot pose, readjusted his balance, and then plopped directly on the ground with a triumphant smile.

"No problem." He put the ice cream to the side and then went to take off a shoe.

"Goddamn it." Rory marched up to the Mermaid, one hand on her hip. She stared at her. Then, with a finger pointed directly at her, she snapped, "I know what you're up to, Charlotte Tuna. And you're not getting him."

"Oh, I'm getting him, Druid." The mermaid winked and flashed a lush-lipped smile filled with razor-sharp teeth. "And you can't stop me." She threw back her head and sang louder. Rory could hear it finally. The singing was indeed beautiful. But, then again, it had to be for a monstrous tart like her to get fed, so Rory wasn't impressed.

Rory was also not going to let her husband go without a fight. The mermaid was correct. Rory was a Druid. She was the last one in the world, as far as Rory knew. And she knew magic. She knew that the mermaid's song, the Siren song, was unstoppable. It had broken many a man and driven them to madness and death by drowning. There was no magic she could do to save him.

But this big-boobed fish bait bitch didn't know her Francis. She didn't know Rory's big, stupid, lovely wrecking ball of a husband. And she wasn't ever going to get to if Rory had any say.

"Whatcha talking about ladies?" Francis materialized behind Rory. He could move quietly when he wanted to, and the crashing waves had muffled his barefoot padding on the stones near them. In one hand he had his sneakers tied together. In the other, he had the melting soup of a banana bucket. He handed the bucket back to Rory.

"Her singing." Rory scrunched her face thoughtfully. "Is it better than Ozzy?"

"Ozzy?" Francis paused and for a second or so Rory saw a flash of something. Recognition? Coherent thought? "Ummm… Yeah, it's definitely better than Ozzy."

"Did you just compare my singing to Ozzy Osbourne's?" the mermaid pouted. "The crazy screaming guy from Black Sabbath?"

"I did. He's one of Francis' favorite musicians."

"We'll see who his favorite is." The mermaid blew a kiss to Francis and returned to her song. It was slower this time. Still beautiful, if you liked mantrap fish music, but it wasn't Rory's cup of tea.

Francis smiled and began to absentmindedly pull his tee-shirt over his broad shoulders. He hummed along with the tune as he peeled it off, revealing his tattooed back. The Celtic knots of strength and protection shone brightly in the light of the afternoon sky. Rory knew that they were working. No knots had been scratched or broken. But the knots protected her husband from physical damage, not mind control from man-eating aquatic whores.

"Hey, love, I enjoy a show as much as the next girl, but…" Rory placed a hand on Francis' arm to slow his stripping.

"Oh, not as much as I am," the mermaid sang with a naughty lilt. Rory fought back the urge to slap the smile off her perfect red lips.

"But, I need to know. Is her singing better than Bruce Dickinson's?" Rory crossed her arms and tapped her foot, waiting for an answer. If Francis could pay any attention, he'd see that she was looking annoyed. He would give her an answer as quickly as he could to avoid that.

"Wait." The mermaid put up a hand and stopped singing and snarled, "Are you actually comparing my dulcet tones to the human equivalent of an air-raid siren?" She sighed and fluffed back her hair dramatically. "You know that's just offensive."

"Well…his voice is as powerful as yours. I mean, my lord when he opens up on *Number of the Beast*?" Francis dropped his tee-shirt onto the grass and tilted his head thoughtfully. There was Rory's husband! A man capable of arguing rock and metal music at any time. With anybody. This had caused them more problems than good and had resulted in the launching of one idiot through a window after the fabled "Sammy Hagar vs David Lee Roth" argument got heated. Sammy won that one. Obviously.

"But is it as beautiful as this?" The mermaid launched into a song of love and loss so powerful and gorgeous that it would have made Celine Dion weep.

"Wow." Francis' eyes clouded over, and a dopey smile formed on his face like he'd spent the night out drinking with the boys. He wobbled in place, humming along until her song suggested he take off his pants. Francis pulled at his jeans' zipper.

"Whoa there, boy." Rory put a hand on his waist. "It's not that kind of party, love."

"It will be." The mermaid ran a tongue over her pointed teeth during a particularly haunting rise in her song.

"Last question, my dear." Rory locked eyes with Francis' bleary ones, trying to burrow past the magic stupor. "Is she better than Freddy Mercury?"

The mermaid music stopped dead.

"How. Dare. You." The mermaid snarled, baring her multiple rows of jagged teeth.

"That's actually a really good question…" Francis let go of his zipper and chewed a thumb. "I mean, I can't deny the power and majesty of her song, but is there a better song ever than Bohemian Rhapsody?"

"Are you ready to give that up forever? To give up me forever? Just for a swim and some tail from her?" Rory knew that her husband loved her. And that he loved his music. Probably in that order.

"No… I mean, I…" Francis shook his head, trying to clear the magic fog like a dog ridding itself of pond water on its coat.

"You. Bitch!" The mermaid hissed and rushed Rory, her perfectly manicured nails becoming wicked curved claws. Rory sidestepped a slash and launched her banana bucket at her face. It exploded all over her, covering her bright red hair, perfect lips, and buxom chest in dripping chocolate, strawberry, vanilla, fudge, whipped cream, pineapple, and nuts.

"I'll kill you!" screamed the mermaid as she tore at her own face, trying to clear the delicious mess.

"No, you won't." Francis thundered toward the mermaid, jeans button undone but pants still up. He threw his arms around her and, in a bear hug, dragged her to the edge of the cliff. Then, with an "Ay-Oh!" he heaved her off the side and toward the crashing waves below. She fell, still screaming death threats at Rory, and hit the water with a loud slap.

"You owe me a banana bucket." Rory grabbed her husband's arm as he shoved his foot into his sneaker. It was the last piece of clothing he had left to put on.

"Sure. But I'm getting to eat it too, right?"

"Absolutely not. You barely chose me over that fish woman!"

"C'mon! That was her creepy magic singing." Francis pulled Rory in for a hug and smooch. "You know I love you."

"Don't care." She wiggled out of his arms and swatted at his arm, "If not for Queen, you'd be mermaid food. No ice cream for you!"

"I'm still getting a spoon." Francis shrugged and reached out to hold his wife's hand. She relented.

"If you take one bite, I'll kill you myself."

"Ah, who wants to live forever?"

About the Author

Brian MacDonald writes in the earnest hope that his words can bring joy and comfort like the books of his youth brought him. He has returned to the writing world after a twenty-plus-year hiatus filled with teaching Intensive Special Education in the private and public schools of Massachusetts. His years with his students have informed his worldview and taught him to take nothing for granted and to see the beauty in the chaos swirling in our minute-to-minute struggles in life. Brian's work tends but doesn't always include elements of fantasy and science fiction as well as dumb jokes and fisticuffs.

In ending, Brian would like to state that he disagrees with Conan. While he agrees that crushing one's enemies and hearing the lamentation of their loved ones is indeed enjoyable, Brian is absolutely certain that "Homemade Calzone" night at the MacDonald house with his wife, sons, and reruns of Leverage is the best thing in life.

Hide Like the Blueies

by

Craig Crawford

Hide Like the Blueies

*N*omi! *Monsters!* came the thought in Sindari's head.

Tending the fish gardens at the edge of the current, she looked up, and sure enough Aeyna was nowhere to be seen. *Where are you?* Sindari thought back at her daughter. Moments ticked by. Sindari's stress increasing with each sway of the sea.

By the coral mounds with the orangies and the blueies, came the thought. *I'm visiting Bemon eight legs.*

Sindari saw the spot where she sat as a flash inside her head. *Have they seen you?*

No, Nomi. I ducked into the rocks just like you taught me. The monsters are dark and scary. I don't like the way they're hovering above— I think they're looking for me.

Stay low and blend in. I'm on my way. If they spot you, yell. Sindari flicked her long tail and fired through the water, leaving the gardens behind. Staying low along the ocean floor, she glided through the water. Aeyna befriended the eight-legs several cycles back and she loved pestering her with questions and playing games. They represented some of the smartest creatures in the sea, save maybe for Sindari's kind and the warm blood swimmers.

Sindari ducked between the coral reefs, weaving in and out of the natural canals carved by the sea currents. She used rock and shelf for cover, her eyes wary and looking above as she cut through the water. Her darker backside usually camouflaged her enough to avoid predators from above, but she understood the implications of Aeyna's monsters.

Of all the predators in their sea, only one threatened them individually and as a whole.

Sticking out an arm, Sindari angled right around a long wall of coral, shifting to approach Aeyna from the back. She knew exactly where Bemon hid amongst the coral mound, and from Aeyna's mental pictures Sindari knew where she watched from. She snapped her powerful tail again, increasing her speed. She veered around formations, careful to keep low to the sea floor.

Slipping around a corner, she sighed, sighting Aeyna's backside. Letting both her arms spread and stilling her tail, Sindari slowed. Aeyna ducked close against the rocks, peeking through sponges and juts of coral. Her dark hair flowed in the current, but to anything scanning the reef ridge, her hair resembled sea grass or kelp.

Sindari slid in behind her, running a webbed hand along Aeyna's slim shoulders. Her daughter flinched, but her large eyes relaxed. She gestured upward, above and beyond the reef. Sindari followed the fingers on her daughter's smaller, webbed hand but she already knew what she'd see.

The monsters. Two of them.

I remember we saw them once before, but far away, Aeyna thought. *They're long and dark, except they're sort of like us. Maybe.*

Yes, my young one, Sindari thought.

They have two tails instead of one. Is that why they're so slow in the water?

Partially.

Questions fired out as fast as Aeyna thought them. *But why do they have one big eye with two more little ones inside. And why do they have shiny bumps on their backs? And what are those worms—are they like the cleaners on the lots-of-teeth fish?*

Sindari slipped in next to Aeyna. *In the beginning everyone lived together above the sea,* she thought to her daughter. *Our people lived on the land under the eye of An. But it was warm, and the harsh air scratched our throats. The great God Ea called to us from the sea. He promised respite from An's burning eye, and gardens of endless food like the corals we live near now.*

Your ancestors chose to embrace the sea and left the lands above. Ea taught us how to cool our bodies and to breathe in new ways. He gave us one tail instead of those clumsy legs you see on the monsters. Ea taught us to hunt, survive, and spread throughout the seas of the world.

But not everyone joined us here. Many more chose to continue to live under An's blistering eye. They endured his gaze, building and spreading across the places called land.

If it's so warm, how do they survive? Aeyna asked.

They build shelters from rock and the earth on the land. They also use plants similar to our sea grass but they are much stronger. They weave coverings and use the hides of animals they kill to protect themselves.

They are like us, then? Aeyna asked.

They were, but staying on land, they cannot swim like us. They are slow and awkward in the sea, Sindari thought. *They cannot go deep, or they die. The big eye you see is a covering to protect their faces so they can see in our world. They bring air down in those shiny bumps on their backs. Those worms are small tubes they use to feed themselves the air.*

Why do they come to our world?

They eat fish like we do, and they like to explore.

Can they talk?

Not underwater, Sindari thought.

Will they hurt us? Aeyna thought. *They don't look like they have sharp teeth. Their hands are small like ours and they don't even look like they have claws.*

No. We are superior to them in the water. They have no claws, but some of them bring sharp, shiny teeth they hold in their hands. They even have tubes which shoot spears so you must be wary of them.

Do they want to eat us? Is that why they're bad?

Over the millennia they have spread over all of the land sticking out of the water. There are many more of them than us. Some of our kind has tried to contact them periodically, but they try to capture us or kill us when they see us.

But why? Aeyna asked.

Unlike peace loving Ea, they are sullen from constantly enduring An's eye. They also believe they are superior and own everything they find. It is why we hide. Look above, and Sindari pointed to an odd shape above, sitting on the surface.

What is that? Aeyna thought. *I've seen those before, but they look like floating rocks. And they're smooth. Except rocks are too heavy to float.*

Sindari laughed. *You are correct my young one. They build things called ships which are light enough to float on top of the sea. They come to our world in those. When you see ships, there are topsiders close by. Not all of their ships bring their kind to swim with us. Most travel across from one direction to another, following the currents. We have to be wary, however. They have eyes they lower into the water to look at our world without entering the sea. They also have ships which can swim very deep. They encase themselves inside hard shells to explore the darker areas of our home.*

We do not want to let them know we are here, Sindari thought. *Ever.*

The two topsiders hovered in the water, swimming along the coral, but they chose another direction and swam toward a larger hill with lots of fish.

Aeyna watched them, fascinated. Sindari kept an arm tucked around her, but she sent thoughts to the others in their colony warning them of the intruders. These two looked harmless enough.

How long will they stay here? Aeyna thought.

Not long. Even with their tubes of oxygen, they can only survive in our world for a short while.

A flash strobed behind them.

Sindari whirled instantly. Behind and suspended above them, two other topsiders hung in the water. One held a round object, and it flashed again, blinding Sindari.

Nomi! Aeyna called.

Swim! Swim fast, Aeyna! Escape like I taught you! She thought.

But Nomi—

Now!

Sindari snapped her tail, and she rushed the two. She rocketed toward them faster than even the beaked mammals and the black and whites. It took only two flicks of her tail to reach the one with the flashing cylinder. A female, she dropped it as she back pedaled, flailing her arms and her legs.

The female fluttered in the water, unable to compete with Sindari's speed. Large blooms of bubbles billowed from her mask. Sindari heard her scream as she swung her arms and legs to get away.

The male yelled too, and he scrambled forward jerking his arms through the water, attempting to come to the female's defense.

Sindari swooped in front of the female, missing her by inches and swum over in an arc. In addition to being slow and awkward in the water, the topsiders had evolved into fleshy beings. Their skin cut easily against coral and rock. And claws.

Sindari had watched several of them bitten by the rock serpents and Aeyna's larger swimmers with lots-of-teeth.

She could have killed the female, but then she would have had to kill the male too. Sindari considered it, but if she killed them more of the topsiders would show up to investigate.

Sindari completed her loop in the water and dove to the bottom. A quick glance showed her Aeyna listened to her commands—she was gone and hopefully rejoining the rest of the colony. Sindari grabbed the cylinder before it touched the sea floor and shot off into the murk.

Returning safely to the cover of the coral, she found a hiding spot and watched the topsiders. The two she had scared swam for the surface, thrashing their limbs wildly to get back to their ship. The other two continued their exploration, unaware of what had happened.

Sindari watched until the two reached the surface and disappeared from view. She hung to the side of the coral watching for more of them, but after a lengthy swim, the other duo also returned to the surface.

Nomi? Aeyna thought, and Sindari felt her frantic thoughts.

I am okay, Aeyna. Be calm. I am watching to make sure they leave.

Did they bite you?

No, Sindari soothed. *I am unharmed. I scared them back to their ship. I will return after they are gone. Tell the others to be alert.* Sindari watched until the back of the ship bubbled and churned in the water. It propelled forward and swung in a slow arc, turning all of the way around before chugging out of sight.

Sindari returned to the colony and found Aeyna waiting with the others. Aeyna swam to her side and hugged her. *I thought they were going to eat you or take you away.*

I've seen their kind many times, Sindari thought to her. *I know how to avoid them, but it is time to extend your education beyond what we've taught you of the sea. You grow old enough you need to understand their world in order to learn how to avoid them.*

Sindari recounted the incident to the two dozen others in their group and they inspected the cylindrical object she snatched. Depressing a button caused it to flash, scaring two of the younger swimmers.

Hels, the colony's lore keeper looked it over. *The topsiders call it a camera. They can recreate what they see through the eye on the backside,* he thought to them all. *It would give them information about us—show the others we live here. It was smart to grab it, Sindari.*

So we need to stay away from them? Aeyna thought.

Yes, Hels thought. *They are very dangerous to us.*

Why? They're slow. You could have killed them, couldn't you, Nomi?

I could have, Sindari thought, *but it would have brought more.*

So? We could kill every one of them. Even if they have a hundred. I watched how fast you reached them. As slow as they are, I bet we could get them all.

No, Hels thought. *Do you remember watching the small silvers as they swarm to defend against the lots-of teeth at the edge of the reef?*

Uh-huh, Aeyna thought. *Are there that many of them?*

Many more than that, little one, he replied. *Their numbers are so vast you cannot count that high. They also have weapons which they drop into our sea and create a rush of water and noise so monstrous it kills everything close to it.*

Aeyna's eyes widened, but she said no more.

Sindari stroked her hair as it billowed around her shoulders. *Our best defense is to hide from them. They do not know we exist except for meetings like today. No one will believe the two above. Hels has interacted with a topsider and reached inside her mind. They believe we only exist in stories.*

Hels took the camera. *I will erase the things they've seen and return the camera to the area. They will retrieve it and find no trace of us.*

So if I see one, I should swim away? Aeyna asked.

Sindari nodded. *You should hide among the coral like the blueies do when the long ones with big teeth cruise by.*

I remember Nomi. I don't like the long ones either. They're fast and their bites cut deep.

Yes. The topsiders have strength but it's not in their individuals. It is their numbers and their ability to attack us in our homes which make them dangerous. They would capture or kill us if they discovered we lived here. But do not fear, Sindari said. *I'll keep you safe. I'll teach you about them so you can survive.*

When?

We will have to be careful for the next few cycles of An's eye. They may return to try to catch sight of us again. But when Hels and the rest of us decide it's safe, we'll go to the surface and I'll begin instructing you, my sweet child. In the meantime, mimic the small fish.

I will Nomi. No monsters will get me. I'm good at hiding like the blueies.

About the Author

Growing up, Craig Crawford read constantly. After being wowed by so many great novels he wondered if he could do it too. In the last two years, he's published thirteen short stories including a novella with four more due out in 2022 including a serial. He writes in fantasy, sci-fi, YA, horror, humor—whatever his imagination gives him.

You can learn more about his writing and what makes him tick at craiglcrawfordbooks.com

Her Skin was Pale and Cold

by

S. R. Brandt

Her Skin was Pale and Cold

As our ship rose on a dark swell, blue scales shimmered in the net below. If that was the fish I sought, the ichthyomagi, gold paled in value by comparison.

"Faster!" I cried. "Haul, you sea rats, haul!"

The nets were full, but my crew strained to give me the speed I desired. We had to have the magical cure that fish would bring and soon—weak as she was, my Molly had scant days at best to live.

I leaned over the rail for a better look. Until now, all any of us had seen of the ichthyomagi was a patch of its distinctively bright, scintillating scales; all we knew was that the fish could be used for healing. We had little idea of what the creature actually looked like.

As our prize grew closer, my enthusiasm dimmed. Though the bright scales were a match, the creature was long dead and incomplete. We had only the rear half of the animal, and that had been hollowed out. Its body was like a bejeweled, empty sack.

A shuddering breath escaped my lungs and my eyes burned.

This last disappointment could easily be the final one.

Only two months ago, Molly was deeply tanned and climbing the rigging, the salt spray in her hair and a knife in her teeth—she was as deadly and beautiful as the sea itself.

I tried not to think about the pale, thin woman who huddled in my cabin, alternately burning with fever or cold and despondent.

I shook my head.

When the net crested the rail, I took the remains of my prize fish, and my crew set to gutting and scaling the rest of the catch. We were, after all, fishermen as well as pirates. Our ship had no cannons and no need of them, for who feared a fishing vessel? If we were stopped and searched, the Tetrarch's Navy would only paw through so much tuna and squid in search of ill-gotten gold.

Ghost Eye and I each took an end of the ichthyomagi and dragged it to a clear spot on the deck. Ghost Eye knelt by the tail and I by the severed midsection.

"Not much left of it, Captain," Ghost Eye said. He poked the tail of the lifeless ichthyomagi with his knife.

My end, the severed midsection, looked to have been bitten off by some larger animal, perhaps a shark. A foot-long mass of thick black seaweed seemed to have taken root in the creature's insides, sprouting from its belly. From one end to the other, the half-carcass was as long as a person.

I studied the severed edge of the creature's flesh—but instead of being jagged and torn, it was smooth, rounded, and straight. With my right hand, I pulled the edge back and, to my surprise, found a row of pearly teeth. I kept looking. There were teeth all the way around.

"This is a mouth," I said, marveling. "As wide around as the fish's whole body."

Ghost Eye frowned and shifted closer. "What's that, Captain?"

"Look. Teeth. And these black strands—at first I thought they were seaweed, but they're part of the fish. See? The teeth have hollow tips and these tentacles, or whatever, come from inside them."

Ghost Eye tugged at one of the black strands. It came out easily until it was the length of an arm, then he could pull it no further.

"Ouch," he said. "The tip is barbed."

He sat back, rubbing his hand. Pinpricks of blood marked his calloused fingers.

I sat there puzzling over the strange fish for several long seconds.

It had no eyes that I could find. Mayhap the tentacles also acted as antennae of sorts? I'd never seen anything like it.

"Well, it looks like this is a complete fish," I said. "So whatever part of it we need for the cure, we have it."

The reason we were hunting the ichthyomagi was that it was supposed to be a cure for any illness. When I'd first seen the thing brought up, I'd worried that whatever part of the fish that did the healing might be missing. Thank the gods of the deep, it was whole.

"The only questions now," said Ghost Eye, "are what part of the animal contains the healing magic and how should we prepare it?"

"Let's cut it open," I suggested. "Maybe when we see its guts, we'll have some idea what to do with it."

I don't know what I was hoping for, exactly—some sack of fluid or brightly colored organ?

Ghost Eye and I got to work cutting the creature open along its length.

"The beast's all stomach," Ghost Eye said as we peeled the fish open.

Indeed, as he cut the pink flesh apart, I was inclined to agree. The creature resembled an empty sack because it mostly was. There were a few small organs nestled close to the ribs. That was it.

"Poor soul," Ghost Eye said.

He lifted a human foot from the belly. The flesh was gray but intact. Its owner had died recently.

I didn't know much about the ichthyomagi, but I hadn't imagined it was a man-eater. It was yet another of the dangerous denizens of the Sea of Magic.

It had taken much persuading on my part for my crew to enter these waters. The foot was a reminder of the risk we took every moment we were here.

Three hours later, at sunset, our cook, affectionately known as Tempest because of her long, wild gray hair, struggled up the stairs with a heavy pot.

My lovely Molly, as frail as ancient driftwood, huddled against me wrapped in blankets. It hurt me to see her so. I'd seen her kick a fully armored swordsman of the Tetrarch's Royal Guard over the rail, now she could barely stand.

"It's not me best, Captain," Tempest said as she set the pot down.

"Medicine often tastes foul," Molly said.

The crew watched in silence as Tempest ladled out a bowl. Molly sipped then shuddered.

"Tastes great," she rasped.

We laughed. Molly finished everything, even the bits of fibrous tongue and ground up bone.

Next, I took out the flute. It was jade with pearls on the stops. The idea of a magic instrument seemed silly, but we weren't taking chances—apart from the one we'd taken by coming to these accursed waters.

Tempest put the flute to her lips.

The flute had come from a ship we captured near the Isle of the Sun. The boat was filled with holy men, their faces painted gold and their hair woven in those ridiculous, elaborate braids of theirs.

We made a donation of fish to their cause—poisoned fish. As the men lay dying, we raided their vessel.

But one got revenge. He hit Molly with a dart, and she fell ill from that day.

Among their treasures, we found our hope for her cure. A basket containing a patch of glittering scaled flesh, a flute, and a scroll that said any poison or disease could be cured by the fish, the flute, and a song.

Tempest played what was written in the scroll, a sound like the moans of the dying. She wasn't a great musician, but she was the best we had. Though she'd practiced this little melody several times over the last weeks, still her performance hurt the ears.

Tonight, though, her fingers danced over the stops. To say she was inspired would be to undersell her performance. She played as if possessed by a musician of much greater skill.

The song brought to mind the ghosts of the sea, women and men wailing for loves they'd lost beneath the waves. Too easily, I imagined myself joining their ranks.

The music grabbed my spine in chill, black tentacles and spread its dark promises through my soul.

"When you play it like that, I recognize it," Ghost Eye said. "That's merfolk song."

Merfolk were the main reason sailors feared these waters. Few heard their music and lived. Those that did, came away with pale, green eyes—like Ghost Eye himself.

Tempest lowered the flute, her eyes round and dark.

We'd come to the Sea of Magic to seek our prize fish. The chance of meeting merfolk was the risk we'd taken to do it— but now I wondered if it wasn't somehow a trap? Why was that song of healing merfolk song?

The more I thought on it, the deeper the chill dread that washed my soul.

What was to be done? I looked at Molly. She was near death. I couldn't lose her. If there was any chance this *wasn't* a trap, I had to take it.

"Keep playing," I ordered, hoping Tempest would listen to my command rather than her fear. "We'll stop afore the sun sets."

Before she could respond, Ghost Eye cried out, "Merfolk to starboard!"

We hurried to see. Heads bobbed in the water, and a sound like the flute, but ever more sorrowful, rose across the waves.

There were so many bodies in the water—like the golden-faced priests when we threw them overboard. The gold of the setting sun glinting off the waves reminded me of the color they painted their faces.

Could these be vengeful spirits instead of merfolk? There were many mysteries in the Sea of Magic.

Regardless of what was out there, I anticipated this would be a long and harrowing night.

"Get below!" I cried. "Lock your doors and stop your ears!"

Molly and I locked ourselves in our cabin and filled our ears with wax. Would it be enough to save us?

I had no idea, but the mere thought of losing her felt like drowning. We held each other as tightly as survivors of a shipwreck gripped the beams of their lost vessel.

And while we held on, the mermaids sang. We heard them, though faintly, despite our wax-stopped ears.

Twice, the music made me forget where we were. I dreamed, or perhaps it was a vision, that we were among the murdered, gold-faced priests. Their dead bodies laughed at us, mirthless and mocking.

Once when I awoke, I swore I could hear a knocking at the door, a faint muffled sound. No one should be about the ship tonight.

"Go back to your quarters!" I shouted.

A long silence followed, then something pounded at the door until it shook in its frame. Molly gripped me tightly. Was she getting stronger? I hoped so.

Regardless, I pulled away from her and readied my cutlass in case whoever or whatever was on the other side broke through.

The song came through loudly now, intoned by deep notes and carried by the vibration of our very bones. The tune was the selfsame one that Tempest had played.

For the priests with faces gold,
For your countless murders bold,
An off'ring must be made,
In blood it must be paid.

The words sank inside me like a rapier's tip, engraving their meanings somewhere in my depths.

I shivered, as though with a fever. My eyes watered.

I'd been the target of a spell like this once before when the Tetrarch's wizards cursed us. Whatever had been on the other side of that door had leached a piece of our souls. This night, as then, it left me feeling weaker, hollower, vaguely lost.

"Leave us!" I screamed, willing the thing outside to be gone.

Mercifully, the music faded then, and the door no longer shook.

I dropped my cutlass and returned to Molly, wrapping us both in a blanket.

All the rest of the night, things knocked about the ship and the song assailed us.

When morning's rays at last slanted in my cabin's window, Molly was cold and stiff in my arms. The cure had failed.

I brushed her hair and tried to weep for her. Despite the depth of loss I felt, though, the tears wouldn't come.

We'd spent many years together, Molly and I—gathering treasure, braving storms, and making love. I tried to remember all the good times. Instead, I kept thinking about the creature outside our cabin last night, stealing the last shred of Molly's life with its foul spell.

Finally, I bared my teeth and snarled.

By the gods of the deep, I would give her a decent burial—and a more decent revenge.

The merfolk would pay.

It took me an hour to prepare Molly's corpse, to adorn her neck with gold, her fingers with rings of emerald and ruby, her ears with diamonds. I dressed her in a priceless silk and fastened strongboxes filled with loot to her ankles.

When it was done, my crew and I heaved her overboard. Molly sank beneath the waves, carried to the bottom by her share of the treasure we'd amassed.

Most religions say you can't take money with you, but pirates believe otherwise.

We watched the water in silence, all of us ghost-eyed now, mourning our losses.

And our losses were many.

Indeed, six of the crew had gone missing in the night, including Ghost Eye himself. The place the six once had in our hearts was now filled with darkest desire for vengeance.

Together, we raised our swords, cutlasses, axes, and spears and made our pledges to the gods of the deep. Each of us, every man and woman, vowed that those creatures would taste steel before they took another soul. We'd terrorized the

Tetrarch and his priests, now we'd bend or murderous hearts toward the merfolk.

To that end, we needed to summon them.

At twilight, we lit the deck lanterns so they could see us, and Tempest played the flute. As Ghost Eye's lover, she wanted to slice their flesh as much as I.

As the golden sun sank below the horizon, a mournful song answered hers. The merfolk swam slowly toward us, arriving at the ship's side as a cloud eclipsed the moon.

I stood at the rail and watched our shadowy visitors, trying to make out their forms in the dark. The crew stood behind me.

"Let us up," one creature called.

Chills danced along my spine.

The voice was Molly's.

No, it couldn't be. This was more of their strange magic.

"You got up well enough last night!" I yelled, my hand resting on the hilt of my cutlass.

"'Twas I that let them up," Ghost Eye's voice drifted up from the sea.

At the sound of his voice, Tempest joined me at the rail, gripping the hilt of her sword where it rested in its sheath.

"My love," Ghost Eye called out.

"What devilry is this?" Tempest asked.

A good question. I squinted in the darkness, but all I saw where shadowy shapes. How had these creatures stolen the voices of our crew?

I decided it didn't matter. We couldn't cut them unless they came on board.

I let down the rope, then Tempest, the rest of the crew, and I backed away.

The first of the merfolk heaved itself onto the rail and flopped on the deck. With the lower body of a fish, she was nearly helpless, wriggling awkwardly on the boards. Her scales flashed like blue diamonds in the light of our deck lanterns, like the scales of the ichthyomagi itself.

"The first one's mine!" I called.

I took two hot-blooded steps and raised my cutlass. It would be easy to slice her—but when I saw her face I froze.

Molly.

Though she was still thin, she looked strong and alive. Her eyes were passionate, dark, and full of mischief—the way they'd been before she was poisoned.

I'd almost forgotten how beguiling her gaze was—just as magical and capable of soul-stealing as any spell.

I took in the sight of her, from head to blue shimmering tail.

It was then that I understood. Her tail wasn't as bright as the body of an ichthyomagi—it was an ichthyomagi. Its mouth wrapped Molly's waist, its teeth held her torso firm, and black cords moved under her belly skin, like puppet strings beneath her flesh.

"I thank you for the offering," she said. "This body you cast upon the sea in atonement for murdering our priests."

None of us moved.

"She had to see you," the mermaid said. "The girl who died in suffering, the one who dwells inside me said you might even offer yourself."

I made an inarticulate sound.

Was Molly still in there? If she was, I'd do anything for her.

"Don't listen," Tempest said. "That's how they take you."

Ghost Eye crawled on board. His lower body, too, was wrapped in the bright blue of the ichthyomagi.

He fixed his gaze on Tempest. "You could offer yourself, my dear one," he said. "Simply jump into the sea."

"No," Tempest backed away, her sword raised.

I dropped my weapon and knelt by Molly, or the mermaid, or whatever she was. I put one hand on her cold cheek and felt her salt-soaked hair.

Mirroring my gesture, she raised one icy hand to me. "You gave her gold to take to the next world, but what she wanted was you. Come with me, my love."

There were too many emotions in me to make sense of. Was this my Molly or her killer?

Part of me wanted to gut this creature, but as long as it had Molly's face, I knew I couldn't harm her.

Worse was the hope.

Could this be what the cure was about? A new life among the merfolk?

I tried not to let my rational mind be swept away, though I doubted reason had a chance. How could I think when I gazed at Molly's cheeks, hair, and pale skin?

"I don't understand." I asked, "What are you?"

"Many things: a fish, a mindless creature of the deep; a god, worshiped by the gold-faced priests; and a girl who chose the pirate's life."

When she smiled, it felt as if her beauty was a net and I a fish.

"Do you know how much glittering treasure lies unclaimed below?" she asked. "It's free for the taking, and the Tetrarch's forces can never catch us. Join me. Become one of us. Throw yourself into the sea."

My response came without thinking.

"The only treasure I want from the sea is you."

I drew in a deep breath.

It would be so easy to obey her, to step over the rail and into the black water, to be with her for all eternity.

No.

I pulled away, stood, and walked to the rail.

I needed to think, and I could never do that while looking at her.

The moon had come out from behind the clouds, bathing the sea with its bright, ghostly light.

Countless heads bobbed on the waves nearby. A few were bald and colored gold—priests, like the ones we'd killed for their wealth. Were they behind this? Were they using my Molly's corpse to wreak a terrible vengeance, or did they offer me a mercy?

"Do you know why the priests paint themselves gold?" Molly asked.

I shook my head.

"To show the value of a human soul, the flame of life carried within."

Almost, I wanted to laugh. The priests thought of themselves as treasure?

When the next words left her lips, they were like the call of the sea when I was a boy, the thrill of blood on an enemy deck, cold metal coins in my hands. *"Dive with me. Be the gold I carry to the deep, and I will be yours."*

Her eyes were dark and empty, her skin was pale and cold, but she was all that life had left me. Gold was dull by comparison to my Molly, and a pirate doesn't go to the deeps without his treasure.

Was there ever any real doubt what I would choose?

"Aye," I said.

With that, I went to her, lifted her in my arms, and climbed onto the rail. The ocean below me was dark and alive with faces. Many arms beckoned to me. Chill air tingled across my skin.

"No! Captain!" Tempest called.

I glanced back at the woman, my friend for so many years—at the ship and the rest of my crew. They were my shipmates, the men and women who'd helped me kill and collect gold. Despite their wealth, their clothes were worn, torn, and stained with fish guts and human blood. There were empty places in their company, the spots once occupied by Molly, Ghost Eye, and the others who went missing.

"I must go," I said. "Whether to find love or death, salvation or damnation, my place is with her. The ship and my share of the treasure is yours if you want it."

With a last smile and nod, I hefted the creature in my arms and leaped into the sea, ready to receive Molly and all the spoils of the deep.

About the Author

S. R. Brandt is an author, father, computer scientist, spinner of black holes, and amateur martial artist. He is a traveler, but at six four, he doesn't fit well in airplanes. Fortunately, journeys to impossible worlds only require mental space and don't require any higher price than the ability to read.

Adapt

by

Jessica Guernsey

Adapt

The NASA representative resisted the urge to clear her throat as she stood before the bank of microphones. Hardly anyone in the gathered group looked up as she began speaking. "Our Jupiter probe made a successful trip around the planet and is now approaching Europa, the frozen moon where we recently confirmed water underneath the ice. Water means there's a greater chance for signs of life." Now she swallowed because this is where she went off script. "We also hope to find the source or potential sources of the signal we've received during a previous mission."

Reporters, only half listening before, snapped to attention.

One raised a hand. "What signal?"

She pulled a small device from her pocket. "This one." She pressed a button.

The air filled with surreal sounds, a sort of mournful whale song mixed with the static of the stars. Jaws went slack as they listened. When the second voice joined in, many in the room jumped to their feet, hands waving overhead as they shouted their questions at the representative.

She smiled.

With a frantic pump from my tail, I hurled into the crack in the ice covering the water. Being slippery helped me wedge myself further into the crevice, the scales on the undersides of my arms already thickening in response to the contact with the cold. My chest burned as my breathing adapted to air instead of water. This always hurt. No matter how many times I forced the air in, just like my sister had shown me.

Sister.

I glanced down at the deep, dark water. No sign of motion. But something had been there. I knew it. I felt it move in the surrounding darkness. I'd never gone that deep before, never journeyed so far down the columns that rose from the depths, flattening in shelves at the top, where we slept and kept our eggs. But I'd had to go. I had to.

My sister. I hadn't seen her in far too long. Like me, she didn't like to spend her time alone, as the others preferred. But she hadn't been on her shelf. Or any other shelf I'd found. No one had. Not a single other had been anywhere I'd searched. There were only vague brown patches, some even clouding the water as I moved. It was why I had ventured into the dark. Where else could they have gone but down?

We'd been warned about going too deep, like we'd been warned about so many other things. We were never to enter the domain of the Far Befores, those that first arrived here, before the light of Father's blessing allowed some to adapt to the ice-crusted waters. Before becoming what we were now. No other really knew what a Far Before looked like. Only whispers of immense things moving. The Far Befores never came up to our shelves, and we never went down into the dark.

Those that went down did not return.

I certainly didn't want to know what they looked like, how our bodies had looked long ago, before we adapted, became smaller so food would last longer, arms slender to help care for our eggs and claws to grip the shelves when the waves roared overhead. I didn't know if the Far Befores had sky-dark hair like ours, streaming from our heads and cloaking our bodies when the water turned cold, as it was doing more and more frequently.

I hadn't noticed when the silvertings stopped running through the waters. I'd been too worried about Sister to consider food as I ventured farther into the dark.

I should have been more worried about the Far Befores.

I had felt more than seen the faint movement of something monstrous as it circled. I had swum straight up from there, looking for the first place where the ice had cracked to hide in. The Far Befores didn't like the light.

The water tremored.

A jet of water spewed up through the ice, close enough that I could feel the power of the spray as it shot into the black sky, the water looking very much like the white and yellow flickers it reached for.

I moved farther up the ice until I could see more flickers. I liked the darker side of our waters. Most of the others preferred the lighter side, gazing out at Father's brilliant light, his red eye watching over us, where adapting was an easier task. But it was much harder to see the flickers. Something about those flickers called to me and to Sister.

It was her idea to sing to the flickers. Singing is how we show our appreciation for Father's light that allows us to adapt and for our continued life. After our breathing adjusted, Sister and I would sing about seeking, longing, finding. Sometimes we sang for as long as it took Father to turn around and we could glimpse Mother in the distance, her hazy yellow light clear even through the layers of ice between the sky and the water.

Closing my eyes, I sang to the flickers, my voice echoing through the canyon of ice and out into the black sky. Seeking. Longing. Finding. But now those words were for my sister.

When I opened my eyes, something had changed

A large, black hole appeared, hiding the flickers. Or perhaps eating them? My breath caught in my throat as my middle shook. First, Sister was gone and now the flickers. I did not think I could maintain life if I lost both.

The black moved, growing in size as it devoured more flickers. I could only watch in horror.

Until the hole took on a decidedly not black tone. Lighter and lighter until it resembled Father's light. Pale and rounded, though looking much more like our columns, though broken and floating. The shape drew closer. Colors flashed as it descended toward the ice.

It vanished over the horizon, aiming for Father's light.

I dove back into the water, holding my breath until I could once again breathe under. My tail whipped the water as I followed the shape's path.

I had forgotten about the movement in the water. I faltered for a heartbeat, then resumed my chase. Surely it had given up by now? I stayed close to the ice, my tail periodically slapping against the uneven surfaces as I sped along.

Twice I caught sight of movement above the ice, redirected my course and pushed harder.

Vibrations in the ice shook the water. The shape had touched the ice. I found where it had landed; the surface glowing slightly from some sort of light the shape produced. I searched the ice for a crack, surprised to find myself at the site of where a big rock had broken the ice many, many turns ago, where the ice hadn't yet fully adapted to the breach and remained open to the water.

Anchoring my tail around crags, my fingers digging in as I climbed, I went higher than any other time Sister had dared me.

The top of my head peeked over the edge.

I could see it, the shape. It was upright on the ice as three enormous arms closed around it. Flashes of light still ran along its face. Large red rings faded underneath. Strange black lines marked it.

It had come from the flickers. I'd seen nothing like it.

My first instinct was to tell Sister. But that thought fizzled into a sour pain in my middle.

I could not find Sister. I could find no other.

And now this.

Had the others been right about singing to the flickers? Had Sister and I brought doom down on our heads?

"Never go to the surface," the others had warned. "Never go into the dark of the water. These places are not meant for us."

But Sister and I had been to the surface. And I had gone into the dark. Was that why the others were gone? Why the silvertings disappeared? Was this my punishment?

I slipped back into the water and returned to my shelf. I rested there at the top of the column, in a space now far too large without Sister. I turned my face away from the light of the surface. I would not think about the shape for now. Not now.

I stayed on my shelf for many of Father's rotations. When Sister disappeared, I basked in Father's light to grow my tail, stretching the blue color to something paler as it lengthened to double. I needed a longer tail to move me through the waters faster, in search of her, in search of any other. And maybe find fleeing silverting.

Once the small creatures had been so bountiful, I could easily pluck one from the water as it rushed past, whenever hunger struck. But now, I counted myself Father blessed if I saw one a turn, far too little to keep my middle from rumbling in need.

Now, my worthlessly long tail draped over the edge of the shelf, listless as my song, my body's groaning demands for food the only sound.

That was, until I heard the echo.

Faint. Just a whisper.

I sat up, listening. It was singing.

I launched myself from the shelf and sought the source, tail working tirelessly as I raced through the water, pausing only to listen for the song. I floated at the bottom of the crevasse as Sister's voice echoed down to me from above. She was on the surface? Sister was always the brave one, but how could she have survived so long on the ice?

As I had done on the day the shape had eaten the flickers, I worked my way upwards, tail and claws desperate on the ice as I climbed.

Once more, my eyes peeked over the edge of the surface. The shape was still there, though it looked like it had grown another tail, a wider one.

My sister was singing the song we sang to flickers from the shape.

I pulled myself up onto the bends of my arms, hair plastered heavily to my body as the cold tried to touch me. I opened my mouth, my song ready to answer her.

There was my voice, echoing across the surface.

But I wasn't the one singing.

My voice came from the shape. It was my voice and yet it wasn't. My voice was still in my chest, unreleased breath burning. So confused was I that I hadn't noticed the movement at first.

A small gray ball, no larger than my head, rolled down the wide, flat tail of the shape, coming to a stop at the bottom. It then sprouted many spindles, using four to walk onto the ice, while two others raised into the air as arms.

It moved toward me.

I wanted to dive back to the safety of the water, to face whatever might be in the dark depths rather than see that strange thing closer.

I didn't move.

Perhaps it was the sound of my beloved Sister's voice that kept me there. The missing of her making my bones ache. And this strange ball might know where she was, might bring me to her.

The singing stopped.

The ball walked closer, pace stuttering. I wondered if it might have trouble moving on the ice. In place of the singing, there was a sort of hushed, rushing noise. Like the newly hatched might make to soothe itself. Was the ball attempting to soothe me? Was it as afraid of me as I was of it?

I glanced down at the water below me.

The ball with spindles stopped.

Sister's voice returned. Only this time I could tell it came from the small ball. Not from Sister. She would not fit in that ball, no matter how she had adapted.

My breathing grew rapid and my claws dug deeper into the ice. "Where is Sister?" I demanded. "Show her to me."

The singing stopped again. And just as before, my voice came, repeating back my words. "Where is Sister?"

My mouth flopped like a youngling seeking their first silverting.

Sister's singing began again, her voice boring deep into my chest and making my head swim with the loss of her. This time, as the song reached where my part began, there was silence.

Compelled by habit, the song broke from my throat, echoing over the ice and into the flickers. Seeking, seeking.

As I finished, the little ball wiggled on its four spindles, the two raised arms coming together to smack their ends. It appeared... pleased?

We repeated this cycle; the ball playing Sister's song and me filling in on my part several times. Each time the ball did its strange gleeful dance and then would sputter a few broken pieces of song in a voice that did not sound like us.

I tilted my head at the gibberish.

Then the process would repeat.

After one round, the little ball stuck on a fraction of a word. "Ster."

"Sister," I said.

"Sister," it repeated in the strange, echoing way it had.

I nodded, then patted my hands together, copying a portion of its dance.

One arm pointed at me. "Sister."

Did it think this was my name? "Not Sister." I hung my head.

"Not Sister."

I no longer wanted to play this game. "Enough of this. Who are you and what are you doing here?"

It wobbled on its spindles, shrinking down a little. Was it afraid of me?

"What have you done with Sister?" I asked, raising up on my arms. "Tell me where she is. Where are the others? Was it because of our song to the flickers? Is Father angry at me?" I breathed heavily, sucking in the cold air as my chest pounded. "Why did you come?"

But the ball only wobbled a little, a series of lights flashing across its middle. The only reply was a garbled mess of the words I had said.

I turned, ready to go back into the water and be done with this.

"Sister," the little ball called, the pronunciation nearly identical to mine.

I glanced back, but still turned away. Sister was not here.

I dove into the water and swam for my shelf.

Sister's song echoed through the waters for many turns after. Sometimes there were interruptions, gibberish and parts of words. It reminded me of when younglings first discovered their voices and began to sing. Perhaps the little ball was trying to do the same.

I didn't want to admit that it was to end the loneliness, that heavy weight that pinned me in place and forced me to think my own thoughts, that forced me away from my shelf. Even if the little ball hadn't understood me, at least it had been another to talk to, something I hadn't had in far too long.

I started for the crevasse.

Nearly there, I noticed a tension in the water. A tremor. It was too dark below me to see anything, but I could feel it there, watching. Had it followed the singing, too?

I paused. The tremor faded, then silenced.

I darted for the crevasse, wedging myself up through the ice as fast as I could manage.

A spout of water rushed from the crack and shot into the sky, as before when I had sensed something. My claws gripped the ice wall as I felt the pull of the water. I may sing to the flickers, but I was not ready to live among them.

As I climbed with my tail and arms, I saw the wisdom of the ball's jointed spindles. The way it moved across the ice made it look easy. Not nearly so troublesome as my current efforts. Perhaps another visit to Father's light would help.

When my head topped the edge this time, the little ball waited for me. It did its little dance, and I had to fight against a smile.

"You come," it said.

I nearly lost my grip on the ice. "You speak?"

"Learn," it said, though the intonation was wrong.

"Learn," I repeated correctly.

It bobbled. "Learn," it tried again, nearly perfect.

I eased myself up onto my elbows so I could pat my hands together. It wobbled and danced again.

It spoke a word I did not know and pointed to itself. Was this its name?

"Eh-aye," I tested the word, extending a finger toward it.

Again, it danced. It made motions toward me and waited.

"Wola." I tapped my chest.

Eh-aye wobbled and then repeated my name.

I pulled myself farther onto the ice, allowing my heavy tail to rest on the surface and not pull me down into the water.

Eh-aye's lights lit up all over its body. It kept saying a word I did not know.

"I don't understand," I said, feeling my face pinch.

Eh-aye stopped wobbling. "From my home. You a story."

That gave me pause. "A story?"

"Yes," Eh-aye said, repeating the strange word.

"I am no story. I am me."

Eh-aye made an odd noise and wobbled again. The sound wasn't like when it tried our language, so it must have been from its language.

"We hear song," Eh-aye said haltingly. "We hear. We come."

I titled my head to the side. "You are the flickers?"

"No," it said, pointing up. "Live on flicker."

Sister was right. The flickers heard our songs.

"Do you know where Sister is?" I asked, carefully saying the words so the spike of pain didn't pound through my chest.

Eh-aye lights ran around its belly. Then an arm extended, the pincher ends rotating. An image appeared, like a reflection on the water. Eh-aye first showed me my home, a ball of white and gray with red streaks, so much like Father's. Next, another image appeared. Black. A white line ran near the top, where a red mark and a blue mark sat very close together. Under the line were several gray lines reaching for the white line but not touching and one rather large green mark near the bottom.

Eh-aye's other hand extended, pointing between its middle and the red mark. "Eh-aye."

"Is this Sister?" I asked, pointing to the green mark.

"No," Eh-aye said, spindles sagging a little.

"Is this me?"

Eh-aye pointed to the blue, very close to the red mark. "Wola."

"Who is this?" I asked, still pointing to the green. "Is this Sister?"

Eh-aye trembled, ran through a series of half-formed sounds. In Eh-aye's limited words, it couldn't answer. But I had a thought.

"A Far Before," I whispered, counting the gray lines between the green and blue dot. Were the gray lines the columns?

"A Far Before," Eh-aye copied.

"Yes," I said. "They are bad."

"Bad."

"Very bad." I lunged toward Eh-aye, snapping my teeth.

Eh-aye startled and jerked back, nearly toppling if not for those clever jointed spindles.

"Bad," I repeated.

"Far Before," Eh-aye said. "Bad."

I stared at the marks, trying to understand why my chest pounded.

"One Wola," Eh-aye said.

I looked back at its lights. "One…Wola?'

"One," it repeated as it moved the pointing appendage across the scene. "One."

There were no other blue marks. One. I was the only one.

I sunk down to the ice; the wail ripped from my throat before I could direct it to the flickers. I had no other sounds after that.

One.

Eh-aye's nubbed hand patted my shoulder, though I barely noticed as my very being felt the agony of being one. I wasn't sure how long I was in that state, though Eh-aye never left me.

I sat up, feeling the cold all the way through my tail. I tugged it off the ice, not caring that small flecks of the silvery blue stayed behind.

"I need the water," I told Eh-aye.

"I need…light," it replied, motioning to a red light blinking on its middle.

My brows scrunched up as I watched the little ball toddle back to the wide tail of the shape and pull its spindles back into itself. Up the flat tail it went.

When the blazing light appeared from the edge of the shape, I knew my mouth hung open as I stared. The ball rolled inside, and the light diminished until it was gone.

Keeping an eye on the shape, I dropped my tail over the ice's edge and let the weight of it help me slide back into the water.

As I made my way to the nearest shelf, I found two silvertings circling each other. I snatched them both and shoved them into my mouth, not bothering to pull off their pointed tails before I chewed. I did not know when I would see another silverting. Best to eat the whole thing. With the grumbling of my middle calmed, I settled onto the shelf, wrapped my dark hair around me, and curled my stiffened tail around everything else. I rested, head full of flickers and my sister's voice.

For several turns of Father's light, I went up to the surface, staying as long as the ice allowed, though I had begun an adaptation to better withstand the cold. Eh-aye still needed to spend time inside the shape so I would rest in the water.

Eh-aye wanted to teach me its language, but the sounds were hard-edged, sharp. I'd have to adapt my voice as well. I'd consider it later, when I was certain I'd still be able to sing. The little ball wanted me to sing all the songs I knew, which I did, though doing so would frequently cause the pain in my chest to choke my voice. Eh-aye only ever waited patiently, sometimes patting me with its pincher.

One turn, I did not want to sing.

"Food," I said as my inside grumbled at the lack of food.

Eh-aye's lights whirled before it said. "Bring me a food. Don't eat. I help."

My eyes narrowed at the suggestion. If I found a silverting, I didn't know if I could wait long enough to bring it to Eh-aye. What possible use could the little ball have for it?

The next turn, I stayed in the water, watching carefully for the skittish silvertings. It took nearly the entire turn. As Father's light faded, I saw the barest glimmer of a silverting. I had it in my claws before the next breath. It was so tiny, not even bothering to jab at my fingers with its pointed tail. Halfway to my mouth, I stopped. Eh-aye had promised to help. Instead, I turned to the crevasse.

The water tremored. I paused, finally noticing just how far I'd moved in my search for food. The water under me, dark and foreboding as it might be, didn't move. Still, there was something there.

I darted for the crevasse, worked my way up the curved ice wall to the surface. Nearly at the top, I glanced back down at the water, which looked much darker. But as I stared, the color faded back to its normal shade. I stared a moment longer, just breathing, before continuing to climb, then rolling over the edge so I lay fully on the surface.

Eh-aye wasn't anywhere to be seen. I wriggled over to the shape. Eh-aye had tried to explain that the shape could swim through the sky to visit other places. Eh-aye said that the shape did the swimming, while Eh-aye sat inside. Its home was a pale blue flicker, and I struggled to believe. If swimming through the sky was possible, I was sure we would have adapted to try it.

I scoffed again as I looked up at the shape. Swimming through the sky. Not possible. And yet, it was exactly the sort of song Sister would want to sing.

At the end of the flat tail, I called out. "Eh-aye!"

After a couple of breaths with no response, I climbed up the tail. I glanced at Father to see if he focused his red eye on me. Would he disapprove of what I did? How I taught our songs to one so strange? It was seeing Father that gave me another idea.

The shape cracked and white light splashed out over me, Eh-aye appearing, one arm waving in greeting.

"Come see," it called, motioning me forward.

I used my claws to pull myself along, my long tail still on the ice as I reached the opening. Blinking through the bright light, I soon saw inside was a large, curved area. A hole in the wall spouted water, filling the curve.

"For you," Eh-aye said, motioning to the water.

"Why for me?" I studied the shape. It was much larger than I had first considered.

"Come with Eh-aye," it said. "Come to flickers."

I turned to look at Eh-aye. "Come with you? Leave here and go into the flickers?"

Eh-aye did its little dance. "Yes. Come!"

I pulled back.

Eh-aye reached out its pinchers to me. "Wola," it whispered. "You are one."

My throat clogged, and my eyes blinked rapidly. "Not without Sister."

I tossed the silverting in the pool and whipped around to leave.

The ground shook, knocking me off the shape's tail and on to the ice.

The shape rocked and groaned as its tails stretched and shortened with the rolling ice, keeping it upright.

Ice rippled under my body. I thought I saw the ice darken, like there was something besides water underneath.

Was a Far Before pressing on the ice?

"Wola!" Eh-aye shrieked at a volume I hadn't thought it capable of.

"I'm here." My voice remained quiet.

It must have heard because soon the ground shivered as Eh-aye's four spindles skittered toward me. It spurted words in its own language, and I did not know what it meant, but it ran a red line of light over my entire length, pausing at a place on my tail. I looked to see what interested the little ball.

It wasn't until I saw the brown-smudged spear of ice protruding from my tail that I understood that strange quivering feeling in my middle. Pain. I hurt. The ice around the shard turned a dark brown color, already frosting at the edges as it froze.

"Don't move," Eh-aye said, hurrying back into the shape.

I watched it go, then looked to Father, his eye watching me. "It's time to adapt, Father. Your light bless me."

My tail felt strangely hot. I lay back down on the ice and focused on breathing as my tail adapted to the wound.

Eh-aye had returned, a small white thing with red markings clutched in one hand, but it stopped and observed my adaptation.

Soon enough, my tail split along the injury. I sucked in a breath. The pain was oddly different from all those times before as when I had adapted underwater. Still, I took in Father's blessing light. My tail split again, and I gasped as the flesh ripped. I stared into the flickers and focused not on my changing tail but on my breathing.

When the hotness ended, I sat up. Eh-aye had crouched beside me the entire time, the white thing forgotten as its lights flashed wildly.

"Wola," Eh-aye said softly. "Good?"

"I am now," I said, sitting up fully so I could examine my new tail. "I adapted."

Half the length it had been before, I wouldn't be nearly so fast in the water. But at least I would be smaller. Instead of one tail, I had split it down the middle into two. I had stopped instead of attempting Eh-aye's arrangement of four. My lack of food made it difficult to continue adapting, even here under Father's eye.

Eh-aye watched as I flexed each tail separately, getting used to the feel of two.

My middle rumbled and I groaned. My arms shook under the weight of my body as I realized just how hungry I was. I collapsed back down to the ice.

"Wola!" Eh-aye ran his red light over me again.

"I'm fine." I smiled weakly. "Just need food."

"Food," Eh-aye echoed, then turned to race back to the shape. It paused halfway to the opening and called back. "Wait. I help."

I listened to vague splashes from inside the shape, followed by whines and strange tones. Soon, Eh-aye was back to me, a strange item clutched in one hand.

"Food," it said and held the item out to me.

The item resembled a finger, though wider and somewhat flatter, and the skin was translucent as thin ice. It was a grayish white color and from one end dripped goo in the same color.

"Food," Eh-aye said, offering it again.

I took it, then cautiously licked at the goo. I looked back at Eh-aye. "Food."

Eh-aye did his wobbling dance, and I continued to suck the goo that tasted every bit like silvertings. When I chewed on the stiff skin, Eh-aye took it back.

"Don't eat," it said. "More?"

"More."

Eh-aye was off and back again quickly, this time with more food fingers clutched in each hand.

I ate them both, though I didn't chew the tasteless skin, handing them back to Eh-aye empty.

"More?" it asked.

"No." I patted my middle. "Good."

Eh-aye danced, and I smiled.

At its beckoning, I followed the little ball back into the shape, though somewhat clumsily as I learned to maneuver my tails along with my arms. Inside, a stack of tubes sat piled on a shelf.

"Food for swim," Eh-aye said, watching me. "Swim to flicker."

I understood. If I went with Eh-aye, there would be plenty of food.

If I stayed here, I'd be on my own.

My throat went dry, and I lost the words.

"I need water. I need to think," I said and turned to leave.

My split tail moved as one to get me to the edge of the ice.

"Wola," Eh-aye called from behind. "Help."

I twisted around.

Eh-aye paced by one of the shape's narrow tails.

I headed that direction, finally seeing all the cracks in the surface. Did the Far Before do all this damage when it hit the ice?

The cracks widened, running under the shape, which was now sitting at a strange angle, the tail whirring and groaning as it tried to adjust, like Eh-aye's own spindles did.

Eh-aye cycled through a few sounds, but I didn't think it knew the words to use.

"Stuck," I said.

Lights flashed. "Stuck." Eh-aye turned toward me. "No swim to flickers."

Eh-aye couldn't leave if the shape was stuck.

A thrill rushed through me. I would no longer be one! Eh-aye would stay.

I looked back at the little gray ball with its lights and spindles, pinchers and all. I did not think Eh-aye would do any sort of dancing at the thought of staying. His spindles, while clever, were not meant for water. He could not swim here.

Could I swim on his flicker? Eh-aye had said yes, showed me images of water, some with the columns rising above the surface. Even some with ice.

But where Eh-aye came from, I was a story, only a song. There were no others.

I peered down at the water visible well below the new cracks. If I stayed here, soon I'd only be a song.

"Push?" I asked, using my hands to shove the trapped tail.

Following my example, Eh-aye pressed its arms and two of its spindles against the tail, making a whirring noise as it strained. We pushed.

Eh-aye stopped. "Stuck."

There had to be some way to help Eh-aye get back to his flicker.

I looked back down into the water. A memory tickled. Of Far Befores and water plumes.

"Get ready to go home," I told Eh-aye. "I will help."

I ignored the way my middle dropped at my decision. Getting Eh-aye off the surface would mean I stayed behind. If I could not swim to the flickers with it, I must take comfort in knowing Eh-aye would sing my songs to others.

After much bustling, Eh-aye showed it was ready to leave.

As I had done so often to Sister, I wrapped my long arms around Eh-aye's body and held it close, until the chill of the ice once again threatened to stiffen my tails. I would need them ready for the task ahead.

"Sing for me," I told him. "Sing for Sister. Sing loud."

Eh-aye wobbled, then rolled itself into the shape. As the brightness grew narrower, I heard the songs of my sister erupting, floating over the far distance.

I stood a moment, transfixed and fighting the spike through my chest. I was one. And I couldn't go with Eh-aye.

More agile on two tails, I dove into the water, waited a long moment for my breath to adapt, then joined in the song.

Seeking. Longing. Finding.

I had sought Sister. Longed for others. I found a friend.

I didn't have to sing long before the water tremored.

A Far Before was listening.

I knew it would. Our songs must be how it found so many of us. With our food fading, I hadn't thought that the Far Before was also hungry. Until we became the prey, leaving behind only the fading color of what was inside us in vague brown smudges.

The others hadn't left.

I pushed down the pounding loss of them. Eh-aye needed my help now. There would be time to sing for the others later.

I hovered in the water, waiting for the darkness to well up from below, eyes straining to make out any form in the dark.

There. A movement. Just where the water was darkest. And getting darker still.

I drifted lower. I needed the Far Before's full attention for my plan to work.

A sudden surge in tremors and a gathering darkness told me I had it.

I darted to the side, bringing more of the darkness out from below to chase me. I was tiny compared to what lurked but in the dark. But I was also much faster, moved easier. I relied on this as I lured more of the darkness after me.

Something in the tremors of the water shifted and my chest pounded, fear making me nearly blind as I knew the attack was coming.

I whipped my tails, angling upward as fast I could. I shot through the water, darkness creeping up on both sides of me as I forced my body into the cracks under Eh-aye's shape, shoved both hands into splits in the wall and made fists to keep me in place.

The Far Before crashed into the ice.

My teeth rattled in my head at the impact. My grip slipped, but I caught it again. I looked down to check that my tails had secured themselves as best they could.

A giant red eye glared up at me.

So much like Father's eye that I nearly lost my grip again.

The water forced its way into the cracks, gaining momentum under the pressure as it squeezed out into the sky.

I screamed as it flooded past me, ripping my hands from the ice. I screamed again as I hurtled deep into the black sky, surrounded by sparkling water that was almost as beautiful as it was terrifying.

Tumbling toward the flickers, my breath froze in my chest. I struggled to find air, sucked in only cold. I didn't know how to adapt.

My home came into view. White gray, marred surface with red lines, just like the images Eh-aye had shown me. I didn't know if it had worked, if Eh-aye's shape had been freed. I hoped it could go home now.

The white gray whirled away beneath me as I sunk into the black sky, my tails stiff and unmoving in this new cold. I could not go home.

Eyes closing, I struggled out one more breath, a final song for Sister. For the others. For Father.

Then blackness. Tumbling and turning in the cold, only barely aware that this felt nothing like my waters.

There came a tugging on one of my tails, like when the newly hatched want to play. My body wasn't obeying my commands to turn to look. Instead, I let myself be tugged and pulled until I recognized that soft whirring sound. Finally, my eyes opened as it pulled me into brightness, then water surrounded me, and my breath pulled in as long and deep as I could manage.

Eh-aye spread itself in the opening. Four spindles anchored to the edges as its two arms had reached greater lengths than I thought possible, carefully bringing me inside and into the water stored for me. Warmth flooded through me, as much from the water as being with my friend. We would swim together to the flickers.

"Eh-aye!" I gasped. "You helped!"

Eh-aye reeled his spindles back to their normal length. "I adapted."

The NASA representative again stood in front of those intimidating microphones. Now the room buzzed with activity as dozens of reporters jostled for position. She held up her hand for silence.

In her hand was a carefully prepared statement from her bosses that promised to not get anyone's hopes up. She turned the paper face down and smiled. "We found her."

About the Author

Jessica Guernsey writes Contemporary Sci-fi and Fantasy novels and short stories (and the very rare Historic Fiction story). A BYU alumna with a degree in Journalism, her work is published in magazines and anthologies. By day, she crushes dreams as a manuscript evaluator/slush pile reader for two publishers. Frequently, she can be found at writing conferences. She isn't difficult to spot; just look for the extrovert. While she spent her teenage angst in Texas, she now lives on a mountain in Utah with her husband, three kids, and a codependent mini schnauzer.

Connect with her on Twitter @JessGuernsey.

Visit www.JessicaGuernsey.com to see an updated list of published works.

The Master

by

Ken Poyner

The Master

I fashion the most delicate things. Intimacies folded within intricacies, gossamer tenderness within metal edges. You would never know I start with scrap; but it is all here: sides of cans, spools of wire, lost nails, spins of sheet metal, the bumper of a '92 Ford.

It does not matter what you start with; it matters what you finish with.

With an array of hammers and bending tools, clamps and pliers and rolling iron, I snip and turn and twist and tether and clip and solder. Each shape I have feathered in my mind and see from the beginning as produced. I then translate it into metal, making the lithe joints and the layered texture of the scales. Each filament of metallic hair has its preconditions, and I bang the shape for some so that the covering will be straight, for others I institute curls. My imagination has already foretold each rivet and bolt and weld before I pull out the first pliant bit of metal, before I start the magical turning of scrap into a serviceable mermaid.

Each one is different, but all of the bent and twisted forms are as functional as my understanding of mermaids can make them. Some are rounder, some are longer, some defy succinct description. I have even tried variations on the hue of the scales. Different shape of fins, ratio of arm joints. And one I gave a single eye, set deeper in the forehead. And no men.

I keep them with me only a few days beyond completion. My work is always the next one. When the time comes that I need my workspace, I put each finished piece in the back of my truck and drive down to water's edge. I start by inviting the salt breeze. Then I bring water to the device, dipping it slowly along the length of the ringing metal body. At the bracing last, I edge in the brute of the fin, and slowly cover the entire fluke. At some point—sooner for some, nearly waist deep for others—they take to the current and, with a curve around the safe and demeaning near waters, are gone.

I go back to the workplace and begin to unroll my scalding imagination of the next. High or low cheeks. Buttercup or watermelon breasts. A broad tail or the knife of a rudder. I follow the image like an abandoned man seeking the shore.

It was months after I had set loose my first, and after I had released dozens, that the mermen came. Two at first, curious only. They waddled up to the side of my shed and peered secretly in at the flash around the open door, as though they could ever be concealed.

I nodded to them and kept on working. I was at the beginning of a mermaid that would in aspect seem perhaps nineteen, impatient and revolutionary; a firebrand that might lead a whole Deadrise of oyster men too far out to sea on merely a dare. There was not much more substance yet to her than a smile and the impression of her littering the air; but they watched me work, watched me with my jeweler's hammer when I set out the eyes and lay them on the table for later mounting, begin on the iron rolling bar to soften the discarded can sides that were to be withered into her fingers. They watched, and then they went away.

Three days later, when I was beginning to overlay scales on her brash and unruly lower extremity, I saw several of them ponderously coming up the small rise that separates my workplace from the sea. There was no hint of concealment this time. When they got to the door, I motioned them in. At first, they would not come, but one did slither a foot or two in, and others leaned out of the light and into my shop's shadow. I placed a scale just so, tapped the flange around its wire base, and then stepped back, pointing to my work.

I think they admired it. I think they understood the art and appreciated the outcome of art applied. But it is not necessary. I work for my own reasons. I would find some joy if they loved my work, but I would work if no one other than me loved it. It is the work that matters.

Some days now there are ten of them, some days only three or four. They watch silently. When the last ungovernable mermaid was complete, they followed me to the water with her and watched as she, more fierce than most, practically burst into the water at the first touch of salt accusation on her fluke. They entered the water after her, swimming at a respectful distance, following her out of the sheltered shallows and into the pound and strum of the open oceans.

I came back to begin another.

A day later, as I was merely pushing around in the air the idea I had for my next creation, a lone mermaid showed up at the shop. Not one of mine, I could tell. A mermaid of actual flesh, one still young but filled with aging. She stood a while, holding herself as upright as best she could against the frame of my workplace door.

After a while, she tilted her head to the side and asked me, "Why?"

"Why?" I said.

"Yes, why are we not good enough?" The edges of her eyes lazily regarded herself before hovering back to review me and the spiritless welcoming space around me.

"Well," I said, "perhaps it is because I did not make you." My eyes scanned the whole of her, and I thought, why yes, I imagine better, I fashion better, I fold and interlock better.

"Mermen, now. Mermen." She slid down the door frame, exhausted apparently from her exercise of semi-verticality. Instantly, I imagined broad shoulders and powerful flukes and arms that could enfold in mastery my mermaid creations, metal to metal, unsounding heart to unsounding heart. My fingers already were tapping out the expanded differences; my memory was replaying the catalogue of unused and available metal; I was in my way forming a face with the back end of an air conditioner housing.

I do not know if she were seeking a counterbalance to the rivals I was creating for her, or a revenge upon the whimsy of half of her species. I could not read her full intent from her drying face, the audacious snarl of gills and air bladder that turned her breathing into anonymity.

She was truly a frail thing. Perhaps stronger than a land woman; surely more graceful in the limits of water; and perhaps an alluring instance as she might eerily swirl by in a roil of seething foam. But I could see she had her asymmetries, her failed balances. Beside any of my creations she would look drawn and weak and unfathomably ill-fashioned.

Even then, I could imagine her as a satellite; as a filament wrapped around something, anything, more substantial.

"No," I said. "No, I make mermaids. Mermaids cast of my fickle imagination alone. There is no greatness implied in their creation." She must not know until the time has come for us all to know, the time of his release, that I could be so easily twisted in my mission, so easily deterred.

My eyes stroked the length of her, and all I could think was counterbalance, call and response. I am so easily displaced.

About the Author

Ken's four collections of brief fictions and four collections of speculative poetry can be found at most online booksellers. He spent 33 years in information systems management, is married to a world record holding female power lifter, and has a family of several cats and betta fish. Individual works have appeared in *Café Irreal, Analog, Danse Macabre, The Cincinnati Review,* and several hundred other places.

www.kpoyner.com

Breathing Underwater

by

Alexandra Angeloch

Breathing Underwater

Sergeant Malady pulled a tangled fishing net away from the carcass in a knotted ball, the black string bunched up like a thousand dead flies sewn together by some madwoman seamstress. Clean odors, the soft brine of the sea, greeted them. Her skin was smooth, unblemished. It must have just happened.

Junior officer Snark gasped and slapped his hand to his mouth, as if shoveling in handfuls of fruitloops. Malady smacked him. "Don't."

"But—"

"Not a move." Malady squatted and ran his fingers along the lower half of the body.

"I heard about things. I heard about—" Snark's words tumbled out like a toddler spilling an armload of blocks.

"Go back to the car. No—don't. Shoot." Malady hated it when he crisscrossed his orders. He had to be careful with Snark. You'd tell him one thing and he leapt and did another. Compulsive. Malady felt sorry for him but pissed off. Why couldn't the youngster contain himself? Malady was 45 this year and everyone seemed like youngsters to him.

Snark edged from foot to foot in the dim morning. For the moment, he was staying put, thank God.

She was beautiful.

Death had not touched her. Sergeant Malady was not even sure she was— He looked at her lips. Cold. No breath.

Snark squirmed. Malady had to give the boy something to do before he peed in his pants.

"What are you waiting for? Write up the report." The spicier the bark, the better the response from Snark.

"Yessir." Snark skittered away, sweating. A roll of youthful stomach bounced over his belt. His blond bangs, combed in a retro 70's side part, stuck to his forehead.

Malady looked back down. Her skin shone pale blue, like the sea during a storm. She looked like a frozen ice princess, made in the weather crystals of the clouds, spun in the heavens, and tumbled to the earth. A bruised blue shone on her lips. Dark hair draped over her shoulders and back. No belly button speckled her torso. Her arms reached up as if caught-in an embrace? Or crying for help? A slight hysteria shaded her blue eyes. Her mouth was frozen open, a look of surprise, and fear, and—

"Help me."

Malady jumped.

Snark struggled with the tangled knot of a pencil string tied to a clipboard and wrapped like a mummy's sheath by accident around his thumb.

"I don't know what to write on the report, sir, I mean, she's, she's a— Is she a doll, sir? Or—?"

"She's not anything."

"But, she looks like a—"

"She's a poor dead woman on a beach."

"All due respect, sir, she is not a woman." Snark pulled at the string while juggling radios, a finger printing kit, DNA slides, baggies, and an extra set of handcuffs.

"Jesus." Malady rescued the radios, scooped up the handcuffs. Snark sweated, his cheeks blooming like beach roses. Malady untwisted the string and set him free.

Snark assembled the loose papers of his report. Malady held his breath for the long, drawn-out oration performed with the Northeastern mountain hick twang to come. "Wha-ite. Fee. Mayle."

Malady sucked his front teeth. "What?"

"I don't know what to say, sir." Snark turned away from the corpse.

Malady sighed. "You're put off by her—" How could he describe it? "Her configuration?" Amateurs. Idiots. How in the hell— Malady pushed the thoughts aside. If he got all caught up in "negative, negative, negative" thinking, as Jennifer called his way of life, he'd never make it out. Screw you, Jennifer, why was he even dating a woman with fake white teeth, like some artificial Greek village whitewash? Jennifer of the perfect world.

"Should we call it a "tail," sir? That's what it looks like. A—" Snark wrote. "Tay-El."

"White Caucasian female with tail. Five-five, tail covering two and half feet, reminiscent of perhaps a large—"

"Grouper?" offered Snark.

Malady grabbed the clipboard from Snark's sweaty grip. "White Caucasian with— Jesus." Malady shook his head. "With TAIL. Not *tale*. Jesus." Why was he so grumpy? He should be elated. Here was some significant find—an evolutionary miracle! He could make millions. There is a yellow brick road, come see the wizard, Dorothy!

Instead, he wanted to punch Snark in the head. Malady had no intention of ever letting the world know that such a beautiful creature existed. Snark would be a problem. And then, there was Sophie.

Sophie, his daughter. Barely 14. Barely dressed. Barely spoke to him. Sophie, whom he was determined to have a relationship with, even if it killed him.

"Should I call forensics?"

"Isn't your shift over yet? Take the afternoon off." Malady ignored the thin ice he found himself on. "Never mind. I'll file the report. I want you to go to the Boathouse Lodge. Lots of vandalism there and— Or, perambulate the docks." God, he loved that word. Perambulate. What a lucky break to be able to use it.

These were the small triumphs in an otherwise tedious day. Tedious, except for—

"But—"

"See if they need help securing anything. The wind's kicking up. Nor-easter coming in."

"But the dock people hate it when we interfere. They hate me."

"Thanks." Malady turned his back to him and looked officious.

Snark trudged back to his patrol car, belly bouncing akimbo. That boy needs suspenders, thought Malady. Didn't these youngsters know about suspenders?

Malady stared at the girl-fish. Salt crystals studded her closed eyelashes. Her look of dismay, and her arms reaching, bothered him more than what she was or might be; who was after her? Malady was a hunter. He enjoyed rooting out the bad people and putting them away. He did not care for the paperwork, or the violence: what he cared about was injustice.

He would love to get his hands on the monster that had scared—and killed—this beautiful creature.

Couldn't you kill them—fish—by leaving them out in the water too long? Not moving? Tangled in a—?

He draped a blanket from the patrol car around her and lifted her up. She was light, almost hollow, like bleached driftwood. Maybe she was a dummy, a doll, like Snark said. It was then that he noticed the red welts springing across her back, clotted with sand and blood. Real blood. A feeling creature. With wounds and flesh, and some brute had beat her with no mercy, lashes through to—

He held her an hour or more before heading out of town. Held her to his chest like he would cradle one of his own: Sophie.

Yes. Sophie. Darling daughter Sophie was another wounded one with a problem he didn't want to think about. One tortured lady was enough.

The mermaid looked a little like Sophie before Sophie's hair turned green. Or, before Sophie herself turned her hair green, then blue, then pink. Sophie's hair was more mermaid-like than the mermaid's, which was dark brown.

Yes, back before Sophie "turned strange" as his ex-wife called it, her hair was brown. Normal. The new hair didn't seem to bother Ronnie, his ex, one bit, but then, Ronnie had her head up her ass, so—

No. Malady policed his own self. No negative thoughts. No diving into the anger. Stay above. Float, as white-teethed artificial Jennifer coached. Ronnie was Ronnie and that was okay, and that's why they were divorced. Now he had Jennifer, whom he didn't want.

Sophie was just "expressing herself" and "finding her identity" according to Ronnie. Sophie had moved in with Malady full time for the summer, sick to death of her mother's false pagan spirituality and bullshit relationship to tofu—Malady's interpretation anyway—and most especially, Ronnie's new boyfriend, Ralph, pronounced RAFE, like the actor. Rafe /Ralph the carpenter/music producer who eyed Sophie with a little too much friendliness. Ronnie chose obliviousness. Malady chose the eyeteeth attack of his side of joint custody and bribed Sophie to come live with him with a like-new secondhand Honda and motorcycle lessons if she was really really good.

Not that Sophie was bad. She just looked frightening and bizarre. She clothed herself in metals and spikes as if preparing for some war he didn't know about. And her friends… Malady did not like her friends. He didn't know her friends, but the little he had seen— They looked crazy too. A few of them had that Roger Rabbit-on-crack look: the three days on meth binge frazzle. He fantasized about personally blowing up all the homemade meth labs himself.

He didn't think she was using—yet. Maybe if she just changed her look. He needed to reconnect with her, find out who she was. That's what this summer was all about.

But how could he reconnect when she wouldn't talk to him? Tonight. He would demand, tonight, a relationship. He would make her steak and eggs—screw the vegan crap she swore by— and he would insist, *command* a relationship into being. She stood stooped, and skinny, and wan. Where was the girl who used to ride horseback and fell asleep at 7 p.m.? Where was the fairy wing wearer who collapsed in his arms at the end of the day? Where had she gone?

A bad short affair, a divorce, and a broken world—that's where she'd gone. The failing grades at school, the closeted demeanor, living for the computer. The not sleeping and staying awake for days with her online friends— She'd slipped out of his grip. He would rip his skin inside out to get her back.

He checked in the rearview mirror as he made his way into the mountains. The creature rested in the backseat.

Snark. He would still have to do something about Snark. He could order Snark to babysit a traffic cone, but that wouldn't stop Snark's big, anxiety-driven mouth.

He drove straight out up into the hills, on a back road with more twists than a head of ringlets, down an unmarked trail, and parked behind an overgrown wild rose bush snaking up two stories through oaks and maples. He pulled the bundle to his chest and stalked through the thigh-high undergrowth. Through an upper country meadow of black butterflies with white dots everywhere, landing on a pile of what looked like bear dung with delighted glee, and through the pine forest to where a stream curled round. He followed it, climbing upwards, into the woods.

Moss embankments reclined like gentile ladies. Mountain snow water pooled over summer hot stones. Mist rose. Too angelic, too perfect, he thought as he always did when he came up here, to his dead father's fishing cabin. He came here when felt crazy. No one else knew about it. She would be safe. He laid ferns down on the dirt floor of the cabin and placed her there. He'd came back later, with a padlock for the door. But first, Sophie.

Malady found Sophie plugged into her computer at home. He was not on call tonight, although his pager beckoned in glowing orange rectangles. Snark would be screwing things up, beeping him endlessly in his quest for just two modicums of peace. Snark would wait. Sophie, on the other hand—

Her eyes, sunken, penetrated the glare of the computer screen. This was her addiction. Not meth, or coke, or heroin, as he had feared, but this. This world. It must end now.

"Sophie." He cleared his throat. He could command an entire police force, but couldn't command his home, his own daughter? "I want you off that machine."

She tapped the keyboard, oblivious.

"Now." He grabbed her wrist.

"Fuck you!" She yanked her hand back and punched him.

Whoa. He released her. She returned to the screen.

Not a good reconnection. He'd let it go for the night. Try again tomorrow. Didn't want to alienate her.

He believed his own lies, found a padlock, and got back in the car. Since the split with Ronnie, the guilt had weighed on him. It was he who had breached the sacred marriage vow. No wonder Sophie was angry. The marriage had so disintegrated by the time he'd strayed. No excuse. He was selfish, but it had become a slow death with Ronnie, and so he breached.

He drove. Night dipped in curved shadows through the hills and trees. A new moon, sole witness, hung above the cabin.

He slipped the padlock on the hook, left it open. The door squeaked. The ferns had browned, curled under her. All was exactly as he'd left it, except for the ferns.

He peeled back a corner of the blanket. Her blue eyes glinted. God, she must have been beautiful, a beautiful—

The Sea—

The door slammed shut. Had someone said—?

Take me to the Sea.

He glimpsed the lake through the crude window. It sparkled.

A Mountain Sea.

Sophie's hollow punch rang in his chest. He pulled out a bottle of whiskey and sipped it.

He looked at the creature. I'll take you to the Sea, he thought.

Tall grass grew in a marshy bank. A dock floated out in the center of the

lake. He waded thigh deep. *Here?* he silently asked her. *Or, I'll take you deeper, past the dock.* He drank some more, a thin stream of fire trickling down to his gut. Tucked the bottle in his waistband, which then became submerged. It felt good to drink and push away the nagging thoughts of doubt about his own sanity, about his place in the world.

The stars seemed to dance on the surface of the lake.

He waited for the voice again. Nothing. Well, who the hell knew. It was probably him, certainly was, concocting conversations that did not exist. He should sink her in the lake and be done with it. She had grown heavy. He pulled away the blanket. She tumbled out, a milky-white blur in the blackened lake water.

It was better this way, he told himself. The world didn't know what to do with such special creatures. It destroyed all things mysterious. He turned back towards shore. Where was the shore?

He searched for the whiskey, couldn't find it. The shore was nowhere to be found.

Damn, the weeds grew thick in this area. Tickling leaves brushed his calves. Wavelets slapped in the wind, set the lake surface alive, as if a million tiny fish skittered just below the surface.

Something moved under his foot. He jumped back, slipping, his head went under a few seconds. Bracing water. As long as it wasn't a snapping turtle. Malady did not trust backwoods snappers, some of which grew as big as truck tires.

He pushed on, half swimming. Maybe the shore was here— or—?

He felt himself grow heavier too. He should have taken his belt off. His gun was on shore, but the water would ruin the leather. He wanted it over with, wanted the girl with the broken back—

Girls, this girl, that girl, broken, punching, wounded girls, he didn't know what to do with them all, wanted them gone from his mind.

Something swept past his leg. Where was the goddamn shore? The sky darkened as he waded chest deep, then up to his shoulders.

Fuck you, Dad. She'd never used such words before.

He scanned the horizon. Finally! But what was the cabin doing way over…there?

He'd swum in the opposite direction somehow, heading deeper into the lake. The dock bobbed a few feet away.

My little girl, where have you gone?

Seaweed grabbed his leg. Malady yanked it free.

His head rang, the shore danced. Damn whiskey.

The weed pulled, sucked him down.

Little angel Sophie.

It pulled on two limbs now, looped around his ankles and gave a sharp tug. The water rushed past his chin, over his mouth, up his nose.

Gone.

He was under.

He met her there in the dank of the lake water. Beautiful. Her lips moved, her hand reached. He had revived her, bringing her here. She was alive.

Her breasts lifted. He averted his eyes. She giggled. Her hair drifted around her head in whorls. She waved him to follow. He shook his head. She beckoned. No. If he stayed under a moment longer, he would drown.

Pressure built in his lungs. Oxygen deprivation. And, peace. His lungs hurt, then didn't, then, scorching pain. She motioned him to follow. He plunged upwards and kicked towards the surface.

His head broke through. He gasped.

Stillness. Not a bullfrog leaped. He exhaled with force, sucked in a mouthful of air, and paddled. Something grabbed his ankle and he kicked it away, hard.

He tried to inhale. The air above the surface of the water seemed noxious. He didn't want to open his mouth. The shoreline danced, beckoned hope.

He plunged below the surface, scanned the muddy waters. Seaweed drifted. The pressure in his lungs pushed, pushed—surely something would burst. And then—*whoosh.*

His brain calmed. Was he breathing? He didn't care. The pain had stopped. That was all that mattered.

She waved. Beckoned to something beyond the web of weeds. She smiled. So alive! This iceberg creature now flipped and curled and bucked her strong tail. She plowed through the currents, the wretched marks on her back gone. She had healed, here, beneath the waves.

She swam into the darkness. He followed.

Maybe she could help him. Help him understand.

He slipped away. He was falling in love, and so things like breathing, or logic, didn't matter anymore.

Daphne laughed. That was her name.

She was showing him something: a place to live, a cave. He was stepping, and floating, on a ridge underwater, when—when his foot slipped. He slid, tried to regain his balance. Something new was pulling him under, something again, had got hold of him. He reached for her, his head hit something hard, and Daphne and her wonderful world vanished.

He woke up, an ache rising at the bottom of his skull. The dank smell of rotting wood, old leaves, mildewed walls, and lighter fluid greeted him. The room spun. Raw edges of an Army Navy blanket grated at his cheeks. He opened his eyes. Upside down rafters loomed over him. He was in the cabin.

Now the headache rang in deep and true, a thousand jack hammers drilling behind his eyes, searing up the back of his head. He turned his wrist to find his watch. He'd been in here approximately one-half hour since he'd brought Daphne—her—whoever—to the lake.

He pushed himself up, then fell forward, his head in his hands. My god, what was in that whiskey? This was something else, this rattling of his bowling ball brain, the deep ache at the base of his skull. The dock in the middle of the lake. Yes. He'd been swimming, he remembered now. He must have crashed into the dock.

And—Washed ashore?

Ridiculous.

He should have sunk, sunk and...drowned.

The Army Navy blanket twisted in a knotted heap. Fresh ferns curled beneath it.

Her ferns. The ferns had he wrapped Her in.

He stood up, steadied himself, scooped up the greenery to toss into the woods, and left. He locked the cabin door behind him.

Snark fulminated boat dock lore and frustration like exhaust from an old Mexican bus. He couldn't get over how rude the boat people were and, despite an offshore steamboat accident which he, as a member of the police force was required to investigate, they would not let him enter their marina, but more important, Inspector Malady—

Malady spat in the sand at the beach.

"Here." Snark festooned an array of miniature liquor bottles and peanut butter snack crackers upon Malady. "These washed up in plastic baggies on shore. Part of the steamship wreck, free goodies for the hotel guests onboard."

"You're not supposed to remove evidence." Malady gathered the bottles and crackers as quickly as Snark seemed to produce them, a stunning variety and number.

"I know how much you like novelty items, Sir." Snark had become tangled with his clipboard and string again, with the addition of miniature cereal boxes and baby Zinfandels.

Malady unwound him. "And?"

The Zinfandels spun to the ground. "The creature, sir? That we found? The wrecked steamship—there was a figurehead carving onboard, a mermaid. In a display with a bunch of other figures. But just this one, this one somehow floated free."

Malady nodded to silence him and pushed Snark's tie back down into place.

"And," Snark continued, "she got all tangled in the steamship wheel which is why she was a little knocked up. But, she was lucky, the statue, making it all the way to the shore. The Pirates of Lake Okenobee display was lost for good. They cost a lot." Snark nodded, wide eyed.

"Statues."

"Yessireebob. They'll be so glad to know we've recovered her."

Snark pulled his clipboard from under his arm, checked items off with his stringed pencil. "I told them we'd get the mermaid back to them today. Okay? I mean, okay, sir?"

Malady swung into the front seat of his car. "No can do."

"But—"

"She's gone."

Snark's face grew red. Beads of sweat sprouted like unwanted pimples. "Stolen? Sir?"

Malady nodded, frowned.

"What'll we tell—?"

Malady waved his hand. "I'll take care of it."

"But—"

Malady scanned the radio call sheet. "There's a domestic over in Scottsville."

"But—"

The ignition rumbled. Malady drove away.

At the cabin, Malady unlocked the door. The Army Navy blanket was folded, and a spray of fresh ferns fanned out from the pink curve of a conch shell.

Is he forgetting? Hallucinating?

Doesn't matter. The woman he meets here is the woman he meets all places. She is here to teach him. He doesn't know about women or how to deal with them. He doesn't know why the aching loneliness grabs him again and again as he tries to reach out and fails. His daughter is the only one he cares about, and "real" women, women who don't swim, and breathe underwater—they are lost to him. They drift. They surface with their bruises and their wounds, and then they float away.

Please, somebody, tell me how.

Tell me how to breathe underwater.

About the Author

Alexandra Angeloch is a writer and actor. Plays produced include *A Day of Wonderful* (Axial Theater), *Bottom Buddies, Cliche Ghost, Beer* (Howl Playwrights), *Making Whoopee, Plan Not 9, Spittin' Devil* (Half Moon Theater), *Old Single Female White* (Great Barrington Public Theater) *Sexy Plexy* (ESPA). Readings: *Siren's Whisper,* (Abingdon Theater), *HERstory* (Howl Playwrights). Published works include *A Day of Wonderful* (Clockhouse, Goddard College), *Butterfly, Breathing Underwater* (Knight Writing Press). Acting: Film: *Night of the Living Jews* (Mama Jones), Theatre: *Remembering Olanna* (Alex) *Ancram Opera House, Season's Greetings* (Rachel) *VoiceTheater, Heartbreak House* (Mrs. Utterword,)/RTS, Emma/ Apocalypse Prod., And a production of her short play *Speed Dating for Unicorns,* April '22, Tivoli NY.

Alex is currently writing a dystopian sci fi novel, *The Partial,* that examines what it means to be human as seen through the eyes of synth scientist and sex worker, Honi Grey.

Tales from Argosy: The Case of the Missing Sea Silk Divers

by

Carolyn Ivy Stein

Tales from Argosy: The Case of the Missing Sea Silk Divers

The second ship in Argosy's city of ships rocked in the gentle cerulean waves, sun-stained with orange highlights as the dawn broke over the Mediterranean Sea. Except for an occasional splash off the bow, the morning was silent.

Chloris took a bite of the salty dried fish she had for today's breakfast and thanked Artemis, mother goddess of Argosy, City of Ships for her blessings. She was on her way to try to teach the raucous children of Hull 37. Unless there were leftovers from last night's party, this would be all she would eat until she returned. She savored it, letting the salt dissolve on her tongue as the pungent flesh filled her mouth, then she wrapped the remainder in oil cloth and stashed it in her cloak.

She picked her way to the upper deck making her feet as quiet as eels slipping through mud. Mornings in Argosy were slow, lazy times and most people were still asleep, wrapped in their bedrolls along the deck and below, each in their own family spot.

She found her mentor, Kosmos, in his accustomed place on the main deck, near the bow, smelling of strong wine. He'd thrown off his bedding and seemed to be trying to rewrap his lame foot, cursing under his breath. She quickened her pace to come to his side.

"Sir, are you feeling well?"

"Do I look like I am feeling well?"

"Your leg again. Can I help you wrap it?"

"Go away, Chloris. I don't need you today. Go teach the brats on 37. Maybe you'll learn some sense."

"But Kosmos—"

"Go! My work is the realm of the mind. Pain means nothing to a philosopher. See to yourself. Discipline and restraint build character and yours is sorely in need of some exercise."

She flushed at the unaccustomed insult. He must truly be in pain today. But if he wouldn't accept help, there was nothing she could do. "Yes, teacher." She rose slowly, making her way to the stern when he didn't seem inclined to call her back.

She felt a sense of foreboding as she released the dinghy and climbed down into it. But that was ridiculous; she knew the sea. Why did it feel so ominous this morning? Some dark magic, perhaps. She shrugged off the weird sensation and stowed her food and a stylus and wax tablet for today's writing lesson.

She treasured floating alone in the dinghy at dawn, the only noise the sound of the sea birds and the lapping of the water. The shush-shush of the oars as they beat through the water and the movement of her arms felt good. Rowing to Hull 37 every day for the last year had toned Chloris' shoulders and arms. What had once been hard now felt easy. But much too soon she would be herding a group of restless children and trying to persuade them to learn.

Kosmos was right. The muscle she needed to strengthen was her will. She'd discuss it with him when she rowed back home to Hull 2 to see what other tasks he had for her. As Kosmos' apprentice philosopher and assistant, it was her job to be his legs, arms, and do whatever other physical work that needed to be done, as well as teach the younger students. The great philosopher himself didn't leave his spot at the prow of Hull 2 where he lectured to her and the other advanced students.

Having made a mental note to ask Kosmos for exercises to improve her will, Chloris sat in the boat mesmerized by the shimmering sun reflected in the waves until a large animal splashed nearby. Her eyes slashed over to the commotion expecting to see a dolphin or a seal. Indeed, she half-hoped to see the dolphin child that everyone spoke about. It was neither.

Looking as beautiful as a naked siren, but far more vigorous, Eugenia splashed handfuls of water over the dinghy, wetting Chloris' carefully dressed hair and getting the briny water in her mouth as well.

"Eugenia, hold!" Chloris said. Her friend executed a perfect curving dive into the waves, splashing Chloris again. Chloris laughed. Eugenia was a show-off whenever she was in the water. As graceful as a dolphin, she'd always been the best at sports and dives. Even now as a beautiful young matron, she retained her skill at diving.

Eugenia stayed down for a long time before crashing up again with a great spout of water. She leveraged herself into the dinghy and squeezed out her wet hair and pulled her arms around her bare flesh. Chloris laughed at the sheer joyous absurdity of encountering her best friend in the sea on the way to school. "Be careful, Eugenia! I can't teach wet from head to toe."

"Your students won't mind. And their parents are suffering hangovers so they won't even notice. Is it true they drink their wine straight? Like barbarians?" Before Chloris could open her mouth to answer, Eugenia said, "Never mind. Doesn't matter. Mark my words, Chloris, you won't be teaching today. Take me to Kosmos."

Curiosity and her old habit of obedience to Eugenia, who had always been the leader in their group of friends, had Chloris turning the boat back. "What's going on?"

"I'll tell Kosmos first. It is a matter of grave import."

Chloris laughed at the elegant elocutions. "Oh, you're such a dignitary now, are you? Can't tell me anything? Out of friendship if nothing else?"

Once Eugenia married Captain Nomiki's son, she'd taken her duties much more seriously. The girl who gladly joined Chloris on her spying missions was gone. In her place, a serious young woman ambitious to exercise power in her own right had taken shape. Aristotle said friendship was a slow ripening fruit. But fruit doesn't just ripen, it also withers and dies. Chloris hoped that wasn't happening to their friendship.

"It's serious. Head back." Eugenia looked firm in her resolve.

Eugenia wasn't the only one with duties. "My dear friend. I am sworn to Kosmos as his assistant. Part of my job is to vet his visitors. I'm afraid that I cannot allow you to see the great man without giving a reason. I wish it were otherwise." Chloris placed her hand over her heart, bowed her head as if in sadness and apology. "Honor calls me."

"So, you are saying that in all honor I must tell Kosmos' assistant about this emergency? Before anything can get done?" Eugenia's mouth quirked into a smile that Chloris could tell wanted to become a laugh. Eugenia wrestled her features down into a frown.

"You have it exactly, my dear friend. How I wish it were otherwise." Would it be too much to sigh? Perhaps. Chloris contented herself with a little wave of her hand, inscribing her sadness in the air.

"Soon Argosy's bureaucracy will rival that of the Ptolemies in Alexandria," Eugenia murmured. "Very well, if I must, I must. Never let it be said that Eugenia, wife of the illustrious Alexander of Argosy, would break the rules."

"Now, spill it, Eugenia, or I'm rowing us both to Hull 37!"

Eugenia shuddered elaborately. "No, don't. Last time I was there it was to remind them of their tax obligations to Argosy. They were…. Well, let us just say I'm not popular there right now. As you are my friend, do not row."

"Then tell."

"Do you remember Tis-as's funeral?"

Immediately, Tis-as's pretty, dark face, with large brown kind eyes came into focus. She had been one of the best sea silk weavers in Argosy.

Sea silk, an extremely fine, golden fabric made from the excretions of the pen shell crab had to be harvested and woven by the same person if it was to have any magic powers at all. Because it was rare, small, and magical it was highly prized. Argosy's sea silk weavers traded it for bags of Roman or Athenian coins. They searched the depths of the Mediterranean for rare tiny bundles of filaments to weave with spells to create truly magical items. A pair of gloves, properly woven and spelled, would not only protect the wearer from poisons, but were light and small enough to fit in a walnut shell when not in use.

Most couldn't weave the spells at all. Chloris had tried to learn the art, but she tangled the delicate filaments, ruining most. But Tis-as took to sea silk weaving like a mermaid takes to sailors. She wove spells into filaments as deftly as anyone Chloris had ever seen. It had been a triple loss when she'd died. Just thinking about that dark day two weeks ago, Chloris felt grief weighing down her heart.

"I remember Tis-as. How could I not? I wish we could have found her body to honor properly."

Eugenia nodded. "Two more sea silk divers disappeared last week."

"In the same area?"

Eugenia nodded.

"A whirlpool? Or a sea monster?"

"I didn't see anything."

"Eugenia! You mustn't dive alone."

Eugenia made a dismissive gesture. It would have looked imperious if she'd been dressed. "I already promised my father-in-law. He sent me to get Kosmos to work on the problem. You know, Argosy can't just stop diving for sea silk. It is too much of our income."

"I know."

"But we can't have our best weavers and divers disappearing either."

Chloris nodded. "If we talk to Kosmos, all he will do is send me out to investigate the dive site. Let's do it before we go to Kosmos. His leg pains him. He's acting like a diarrhetic seagull calling his complaints loudly to me."

"I've never known Kosmos to complain."

"You are not his loyal assistant."

Eugenia cocked her head in a moment's thought. Her eyes twinkled. Chloris knew the expression. It was the same one that flitted across Eugenia's face whenever she proposed an adventure. "Let's do it! You row. I'll navigate."

As they rowed, Eugenia told Chloris of everything she'd seen on the sea floor. She'd dived twice before but didn't see anything out of the ordinary except an old shipwreck on her third dive.

Once Eugenia navigated to the location, Chloris stripped out of her clothes and unpinned her hair, carefully wrapping the gold filigree pins in her shawl, folding her clothing, and stowing everything in the prow of the dinghy. By the time she was naked, Eugenia was already in the water. Chloris joined her, letting the water fly around her as she leaped in.

Chloris exulted in the cool joy of an early morning dive, her body softening and relaxing in the water. It had been too long. When they were girls together, they'd started their mornings swimming before the adults woke up. Now that she was an adult, she missed the simple glories of life.

She let the buoyancy of the waves carry her for a bit, feeling weightless; free, as if she were a dolphin herself. Eugenia soared past her like a beautiful fish. Chloris followed, watching the light fade as they descended, feeling the pressure of the water against her skin and in her ears. Time slowed. Her heartbeat pounded evenly and slowly.

Chloris spotted the shipwreck on the sea floor a moment before Eugenia pointed it out. It was one of the small, flat Egyptian river boats with a single sail. This one had broken up, and it's sail looked like it had almost completely rotted away, but the staves of the hull were indistinct, as if they were obscured by underwater fog. Was it a spell? Times like this she wished she had listened closer to Kosmos' lectures on old magic.

What drove the small boat into the middle of the Mediterranean? Typically, they sailed along the rivers or the coast. It was risky enough there.

She said a brief mental prayer for the crew of that ship, asking Poseidon to see to it that they found their way to the afterlife of the god they worshipped. Who knew if their god could find them so far from Egypt.

As they approached, she realized the boat was wrapped in bundles of filament. She'd never seen so much sea silk. It looked like great balls of wool. Colorful damselfish and wrasse fish flitted in and out of the wreck and Chloris thought she spotted a small octopus before a cloud of dirt in the water obscured it.

Chloris' muscles in her arms and legs burned as the air staled in her chest. She signaled to Eugenia. Eugenia nodded and signaled she would follow. No one could hold their breath as long as Eugenia. If she hadn't been destined for leadership, she would have made an excellent silk diver herself. If she were patient enough to do the weaving as well as the diving.

Chloris pushed up to the surface to get a breath, treading water as she waited for Eugenia to join her.

The minutes passed with no Eugenia. Even Eugenia couldn't hold her breath this long. Chloris' mouth filled with sour vinegar and her stomach burned.

Where was Eugenia? Help me, Poseidon. Guide me to her.

She dived, heading straight for the shipwreck, feeling that something had gone quite, quite wrong. Then she saw the stream of blood and the fish attracted by it gathering in little colorful clumps of shimmering blues, greens, and reds.

She followed. Dreadful certainty crept into her soul, but she prayed she was wrong. Eugenia couldn't be dead.

She thought she spotted someone, but it wasn't Eugenia. Instead, a beautiful woman with long golden hair the color of sea silk floated slowly through the shipwreck dragging something. A large fish for dinner, perhaps? She was heading toward a dark cave.

Chloris' eyes adjusted to the deep-water gloom. She peered intently. No. Not a woman. Not quite. Where her legs should be, a shimmering green fish tail propelled her through the water.

Chloris cringed back, wrapping her arms around her belly. Her pulse raced. Her fingers trembled. A voice inside her screamed at her to run.

It was a siren, one of the deadliest beings of the sea. And she had Eugenia.

Eugenia's limp body bled copiously from three jagged tears in her shoulder and more worrying, she wasn't moving. The trident that speared her lay neatly on the rail of the shipwreck.

Chloris swam closer.

Incredibly she saw little bubbles of air escaping from Eugenia's mouth. Her eyes were open, darting back and forth in terror like a speared fish.

But, she lived. For how much longer? Clearly Eugenia had gone limp to save energy to give herself time to make her move. Her eyes lit on Chloris and nodded toward her, command in her eyes.

Chloris motioned toward the trident and Eugenia signaled with one finger her approval.

A school of fish chased after the mermaid, obviously wanting their part of her prey. Chloris hid herself within their ranks long enough to seize the trident where it lay.

She closed the distance to the mermaid, intending to threaten her with the trident but as they approached the cave, she nearly gasped. Whatever god watched over her pressed his finger on her lips, keeping the air within her. Surely without divine intervention she would have released all the air in her body in shock.

Within the grotto an elaborate labyrinth of houses made from wrecked ships, barrels, amphorae, and bones went on for miles. It must be as big as Pompeii. But monstrous. Hideous. This wasn't just a random mermaid spearing sea silk divers. This was a city of the evil beings. That must be what the divers had stumbled into. An entire city of mermaids and mermen hidden in an undersea grotto. Even if she had all the fighters from Argosy at her back, there were too many to fight.

Her pulse sounded loud in her ears as her heartbeat sped up.

Not good. If she couldn't relax, she'd run out of air before she could help Eugenia.

But how to help her? Could the merpeople be reasoned with? She'd never heard that they ate people. Though why else would they pull sailors down to drown them?

She spent a few precious moments mentally reciting the nursery rhymes she used to calm the children she taught. The same calming rhythms worked on her as well.

She swam forward, trying to maintain the same distance between herself and the mermaid as she ran scenarios through her mind, but the mermaid was made for this environment and she was not.

Then she saw it. As awful as an entire city of mermaids was, that wasn't the worst. In a caged portion of the grotto she saw a pile of human bones presided over by an enormous white and green sea dragon. It stared straight at Eugenia and made a high pitched clicking sound as if it couldn't wait for its supper.

The mermaid wasn't going to eat Eugenia. She was going to feed her to the dragon.

Time's up for clever plans. She had to get Eugenia to the surface before both of them became dragon food.

She leveled the trident, aimed it straight at the mermaid, and flung it hard into the water.

It missed. Even using all her strength the water slowed it and diverted it from her target. Chloris watched it sail past the mermaid's shoulder and straight into the grotto.

The mermaid turned, her eyes bulging like a surprised fish.

All Chloris had left was surprise and bold action. She lunged for Eugenia, grabbed her by the ankles, and pulled her from the bewildered mermaid's hands. Then she swam as fast as her body could carry her, propelling Eugenia to the surface with her.

Help me. Help me. Help me. She prayed to any nearby gods, hoping one would hear her.

Chloris would never know which god or goddess reached a hand to aid her but as she prayed for help, a sudden surge of strength rushed through her limbs. Eugenia's body felt light and tingled. The resistance of the water disappeared. Perhaps she became a dolphin or a whale for there was no other explanation for her power in the water or the way the mermaid fell away from her.

She reached the surface and took a deep breath into her aching chest. Then she swam toward the boat, with Eugenia's limp body in tow. She threw Eugenia into it, clambering in after. She'd once seen her mother revive a drowned child by pressing the child's stomach and breathing into her mouth. She tried it with Eugenia continuing on until her friend finally began to choke and pushed her away.

Eugenia lived.

In that moment of relief, Chloris' mind and body relaxed. The gods released her. Her body felt boneless, like a clay puppet no longer held by string. She collapsed in the dinghy and the world went black, buzzing briefly in her ears.

When she regained consciousness, she saw Eugenia hugging herself around the waist. Tears coursed down her cheeks and long sobs wracked her body.

Chloris rose and rushed to her side. "My sweet friend," she said. She wrapped her arms around Eugenia, hugging her and kissing her cold cheeks. "It's ok now. You are ok. I'm ok. See?"

"It's not that."

"What is it then?"

"I saw Tis-as's pendant, the one she always wore, in the dragon's cage." She sobbed again as if she could no longer control it. "The dragon ate her. That horrid beast ate all of them."

Chloris stroked her friend's hair. "Did you think we'd find them alive? After all this time?"

Eugenia sobbed, not deigning to answer. Chloris knew Eugenia always believed the best of people and situations. She was the one who never lost her optimism. It was her one weakness. She was too good. Eugenie had thought they'd find the divers alive somewhere.

Chloris caressed her in silence until the sun rose high in the sky and Eugenia had released all her grief. It was an appropriate dirge for the murdered divers. Chloris wished she could give them as much, but her heart felt numb.

No one cared that Chloris hadn't arrived to teach on Hull 37. Nor did they seem to mind when she was gone the next day. She wasn't sure what Eugenia told her father-in-law but the next day he'd ordered the two of them to sit with old Themistocles, the mapmaker, and his apprentice to chart the site. It took hours of staring at the charts and trying to understand how the scribbles on papyrus indicated location.

When she returned to Hull 2, she found Kosmos asleep in his place. A flask of wine near his head smelled of strong, bitter herbs. Someone had wrapped his leg carefully in tight bandages. His wife must have taken pity on the old man's pain. Chloris wasn't sure how he'd become lame or when, but sometimes the pain overcame him as it had lately.

She knelt, kissed him gently on the forehead, and sat, wrapping her shawl tightly around her shoulders. The sun was as warm as any other summer day in the Mediterranean, but she felt cold from the inside out.

About the Author

Carolyn Ivy Stein writes time travel, mystery, fantasy, and romance stories. They appeared in WMG's *Winter Holiday Spectacular 2021*, JewishFiction.net, and can be found in her collections, *Lightning Scarred and Other Stories* and *Sweet Lifts*.

She received nine Honorable Mentions from the Writers of the Future Contest. With her husband, Stephen Stein, she writes RPG supplements. Their upcoming book, *GURPS: Biremes and Triremes* will be out in late-2022 from Steve Jackson Games. When not writing, she plays games, hikes, and conducts dubious experiments trying to replicate historic cuisine.

Find her at www.carolynivystein.com.

Chetwood's Unfortunate Connexion

by

Barton Paul Levenson

Chetwood's Unfortunate Connexion

Roger Chetwood came to us very well recommended. He had been a sailor in the merchant marine, but after surviving a terrible shipwreck, and stranding on the proverbial desert island, he had found work on the docks and studied mathematics and bookkeeping on his own.

Now he was Chief of Accounts at Addicock, Ludsthorpe, and Gerville, Shipping and Freight, Ltd. The year was 1864. The Americans had blockaded the rebel south, and as a result, American cotton no longer came to Britain. And Addicock, Ludsthorpe, and Gerville had already decided not to buy Confederate cotton. The firm was not yet in a bad way, but soon would be if things went on the same.

Now you must understand that our President and Founder, Sir John Addicock, was a liberal who had voted for Palmerston. Sir John looked very much the prosperous English lord—stout, fiftyish, with muttonchop side-whiskers. He wore the best waistcoats and carried a mahogany walker with a substantial topaz in the head—the Tiger's Eye of Bengal.

But he had been greatly influenced by such thinkers as *Messieurs* John Stuart Mill and Robert Owen. He had on occasion presented the firm with the most radical ideas, which, on being implemented, always seemed to better the firm's books. The workers enjoyed an eight-hour day. The humblest received a pension on retirement. And Sir John would do no business with the Confederates, even surreptitiously, though we could easily have gotten away with it. He was a firm Abolitionist. I agreed with him on that, though not, of course, to the extent of believing the poor Negro the equal of a European!

But this time we were unprepared for Sir John's idea. "Gentlemen, it seems no fewer than 97% *per centum* of the linen goods we ship are purchased by the ladies. It would not hurt us to have a woman's point of view on the sort of thing we should carry, or even where to get it. And, you know, I have always maintained we waste a valuable resource by not making more use of the intellect of the nation's female citizens."

"Such as it is," Ludsthorpe muttered. Addicock's surviving partner was a tall, thin man, who wore a monocle and, when outside, a top hat. He was quite the reactionary, having stood for parliament to campaign against the Reform Bills. But he always supported Sir John.

The latter continued. "I therefore propose to hire a woman as a route and contract advisor for our growing Asian market."

"Good Lord, Sir John," Marcheford said. "Not for the board, surely?"

"Yes, Marcheford, for the board," Sir John said.

It was at this point Chetwood raised his hand.

Now, you will remember that Chetwood was of humble beginnings. Nonetheless, for one of his station, you couldn't have found a more pleasant, well-informed, and courteous colleague. He was always polite to the ladies and friendly with the fellows, and a fine companion for a business trip or night at the theatre.

"I think it's a bad idea, Cap'n," he said. "Women on a ship—it's unlucky."

Sir John looked at him curiously. "Mister Chetwood, this isn't a ship we are on. Are you quite all right?"

I viewed myself as rather Chetwood's patron, for there were those in the firm who had opposed elevating him to the board. "Sir John," I said. "I think, perhaps, Chetwood was being ironic. He was perhaps worried about an English lady traipsing about the high seas to find out Asian markets. Terrible notoriety if something were to happen to her, don't you see."

"Oh, I see, I see," Sir John said. "Commendable thinking, Chetwood. But, as a matter of fact, the lady will be employed here in our London office. Oh, and gentlemen, be prepared—she is not English."

"Not English?" Ludsthorpe said. He removed his monocle and began polishing it with his handkerchief—something he did only when distressed. "Do please tell me she's Scots or…or German, or French, or from some respectable country."

"It is indeed respectable, Henry, old boy," Sir John said with a grin. "A most ancient country indeed. She is a Chinese!"

At this the board erupted into chaos, everyone talking at once. Sir John let it go on a minute. Board meetings followed Robert's Rules of Order, but often, if no visitor were present, descended into Liberty Hall. But when Sir John raised his cane, all horseplay ceased.

He did so now. The last person talking, caught unawares because he faced the table's foot to address the man beside him, was Coddington in shipping. He was saying, "This humble coolie hope new Chinee-women makee good English jaw-jaw, or honorable board not have good—"

"If you've quite finished, Coddington?" Sir John said mildly.

Coddington turned around and turned red. "Sir John," he said, laughing weakly. "Ah… Terribly sorry, sir. Oh, my. I, ah… I do apologize…"

"Her jaw-jaw is quite perfect, as I know from having spoken with her," Sir John said. "She is a graduate of Cheltenham. And in addition to the Queen's English and her native Chinese, she speaks fluent Portuguese, Dutch, and Malay."

"Portuguese…and *Dutch?*" Chetwood said next to me.

He sounded so strained, I turned to see what was the matter. The man had gone pale and was sweating.

"Surely you know those two nations have many interests in Asia, Chetwood," Sir John said. "I say, Chetwood? Are you quite all right?"

Chetwood gulped. "I seem to have…come over all queer for a moment. I do apologize."

"Nothing to be sorry for, man. Could someone pour for Mr. Chetwood? I hope you are not a teetotaler, Chetwood?"

"No sir."

After the meeting, I said, "You sure you'll be all right, old man? You looked quite ghastly for a moment there."

"Oh, perfectly," Chetwood said. He smiled weakly. "Sorry about all that. I must have seemed a perfect fool."

"Not at all. Happens to the best of us."

We still heard voices in the board room. Someone asked, "And what is this paragon's name, Sir John?"

"She is Miss Tuan," he said.

At the mention of the name, Chetwood turned white again. "No," he breathed.

"Given name?" the questioner asked.

"Qingzhao," Chetwood said.

"It believe it is 'Ching Shau'," Sir John said.

I stared at Chetwood. "Now how the devil did you know that?"

He declined to answer.

"Oh, good heavens. You were a sailor! A girl in every port, they say. Miss Tuan is an old flame?"

"'Fraid so, Cecil," Chetwood said. "Please don't give me away."

"Do my best. Only, be sure not to give *yourself* away! Don't get the wind up when Sir John introduces her." I thought for a minute. "She has no reason to do you harm, does she?" I said. "Parting wasn't too ugly, I hope?"

He looked thoughtful. "I don't think so. I…I hope not."

"Well," I said. "After all, even if she bears you some grudge, what's she going to do about it? Poison your tea? I promise never to let her near Missus Norbury's tea things."

He clapped me on the shoulder. "Thanks, Cecil. I don't know what I'd do without you."

"Go to sea again and discover a new continent, no doubt."

He shuddered. "Anything but."

Miss Tuan arrived by coach two days later, in a fine dress of dove gray, with subdued silver jewelry. I was surprised how uncommonly comely she was, as my taste in women has always rather run to the English Rose. But Miss Tuan was a beauty in no uncertain terms, with lustrous black hair, elegantly coiffured in the French fashion.

At the board meeting, Sir John introduced her, then asked her to say a few words.

She stood up. "Gentlemen, I am more grateful than I can say for your indulgence in suffering my presence here, and I only hope

I may do your great firm some positive good. I am very conscious of my limitations in being both a woman and of Chinese race, and I will most certainly defer to older and wiser heads in any important decision."

Ludsthorpe stood up. I feared the old reactionary might make a scene, but I was quite wrong.

"My dear," he said, "I think I speak for us all when I say that I am charmed by your presence. I have no doubt you will be of great utility to the firm."

Miss Tuan clasped her hands together and bowed in the Chinese manner. "I am most grateful for your support and indulgence, Mister Ludsthorpe. My patron, Lord Addicock, has always spoken of you with the highest regard."

"Hm," Ludsthorpe said, with a quick smile toward Sir John. "Thank you, Miss Tuan." He sat down again.

And then she turned toward Chetwood. "You are, I think, Mister Chetwood, of the Accounts Department?"

For a moment Chetwood looked almost as if he would deny it. Then he said, "Yes. Ah, yes. Roger Chetwood, Miss Tuan. Pleased to…make your acquaintance."

"I believe we have met before, sir, in the vicinity of Macau," she said. "I hope I might call upon you on some occasion, properly chaperoned, of course, to talk over old times. Would that be acceptable to you, sir? I do not mean to be forward and hope you will not take it as such."

"No. Ah, no," Chetwood. "I mean, of course not. Not forward, I mean."

"Then I might do so?"

"I… Ah, not, not at present. I am rather busy of late."

"At your leisure, then, sir." She turned to Sir John. "I do apologize for pursuing an irrelevance in the course of a business meeting. Gentlemen, I am most honored to make the acquaintance of each and every one of you." She sat down again.

During the full minute of applause the board gave her—in which I joined—I recalled that Chetwood had been shipwrecked off Macau.

It was not long before Miss Tuan had the firm of Addicock, Ludsthorpe, and Gerville firmly under her thumb. Her suggestions on where to secure inexpensive cotton and other *matériel* in China, in the newly-opened Japan, and, of course, in India, all proved sound. Money almost flooded back into the firm.

She made suggestions everywhere, in every department. You might think I describe a typical meddling female, but she was nothing of the sort—she only made suggestions, gently and tentatively. And she did so in such a way that whomever she spoke to took it as an opportunity to discourse on his own specialty. She listened with great fascination, looking up at the speaker with wide eyes. She only said a few admiring words here and there, yet somehow the fellow always wound up adopting her suggestion.

And she was a shameless manipulator. Marcheford, our chief buyer, was—Heaven help us—what they call a "freethinker." When Miss Tuan asked him why we bought automated looms from the firm of Krupp, Thyssen and Zerstörte, when we could get less expensive ones from Lefevre and Broussard, he replied that it was because of "German engineering. Can't beat the Germans for that sort of thing! And Lefevre and Broussard—well, French, you know. One doesn't expect precision engineering from the French."

"Oh, I see," Miss Tuan said. "It is a religious matter, then?"

"What?"

"Something to do with religion? I have not yet fully understood all your English customs and manners, but I completely respect—"

"What the devil has religion to do with it?"

"I thought perhaps you had in mind the Protestant work ethic. The Germans are, of course, primarily Lutherans, whereas the French are Roman Catholic. And England, of course, is thoroughly Protestant. Perhaps you fear public opinion if you were to buy from a French firm?"

"What the devil! I don't fear any such thing!"

"I did not mean you personally, of course! I merely—"

"If I make a recommendation, the firm agrees," Marcheford said. "I have never yet been overruled on a purchasing decision."

"Oh! They must respect your opinion greatly. I do myself, so I can certainly see—"

"Look, Miss Tuan, you just send me the plans and specifications for the French machine. I shall look them over and make an objective decision, a decision based purely on reason, you understand."

"Thank you, sir, I shall certainly do so."

The only man with whom she could make no headway was Chetwood. I don't mean to say he was impolite, or bluntly turned her down. He would only listen patiently, saying next to nothing and nodding all the while, and then change nothing. Miss Tuan never liked to show any side of herself but the most cheerful and subservient, but on more than one occasion I saw her turn away from Chetwood with intense frustration on her pretty face.

A number of us met at the Dorset Thursdays for a mid-day dinner. They allow anyone respectable in the doors, but there is no atmosphere of oppressive formality; though they have a very good wine list, a gentleman can also order a pint of bitter if so inclined.

I was first in that day. The place has wonderfully unique decoration. Amidst the tables stand no fewer than a dozen great hexagonal fish tanks of green glass, each with live game fish or lobster in its depths—and the patrons are invited to pick out their choice of individual on which to dine! I always had the turbot at the Dorset—the chef makes a wonderful turbot, with herbs and a sauce in the French manner.

William seated me, and I was surprised to see an extra place set. "I say, whose is that?" I asked.

"Mister Ludsthorpe has requested an additional place setting, sir."

"Oh! Must have a guest. I wonder who? Or is it whom?"

"Will you be having your usual, sir?"

"Not till the others arrive, but yes."

"A drink in the meantime, sir? Some oysters?"

"That sounds fine."

Marcheford came in next, then Harrington, McTaggart, and Chetwood. We all greeted one another warmly, congratulating Bert McTaggart, whose son had entered the Coldstream Guards. Then

Ludsthorpe came in—reactionary old Ludsthorpe, the man who opposed the reform bills and thought woman suffrage a joke—and on his arm walked none other than Miss Chingshau Tuan!

Chetwood stood up. We all followed. I then realized Chetwood had shot to his feet, not out of politeness, but something more akin to shock. "You can't be serious!" he told Ludsthorpe. "You bring a woman in here?"

Miss Tuan looked stricken but tried to conceal it. Ludsthorpe merely raised one eyebrow. "Women are not, I believe, barred from the Dorset, Chetwood," he said. "And Miss Tuan...is a *lady*."

Chetwood utterly lost his head. "Don't you see what she's doing?" he said. "She's taking over! She'll be running the firm like a queen inside a year because none of you have the brains to see—"

"Chetwood!" Ludsthorpe said. "Please control yourself! I do not understand, nor do I appreciate, your antipathy to Miss Tuan. Whatever, er, history the two of you may share is no concern of this firm and no reason for unprofessional behaviour!"

"She's not human! *She's not even human!*"

"I hope you're speaking figuratively," Marcheford said. "But if you're referring to her being Chinese, you are quite mistaken. I don't know how much you know about the science of Man, Chetwood, but whether one follows the polygenists or the monogenists, the Chinese are certainly—"

"I'll *show* you," Chetwood said, his teeth gritted.

"For God's sake, Roger," Miss Tuan said. "I'm not here to threaten you. I just came in for lunch!"

Chetwood grabbed his wine glass from the table. He turned to the nearest fish tank and scooped up water.

Ludsthorpe said, "Chetwood, I tell you right now that if you have any idea of heaving that glass at Miss Tuan, not only will I horsewhip you, but you will never work at Addicock, Ludsthorpe, and Gerville again."

Chetwood turned back to us. "I'm not throwing the glass," he said.

He tasted the water.

"Good Lord, Chetwood, that stuff must be filthy!" Harrington said.

"Salt," he said. "It's salty. That's the point." He put the glass down, turned again, and with a strength I did not know he possessed, grabbed the legs of the table supporting the fish tank and upended it.

"No!" Miss Tuan screamed.

"CHETWOOD!" Ludsthorpe shouted.

Chetwood had chosen his direction carefully. Water and fish cascaded over Miss Tuan.

She gave out a shriek to pierce the heart and fell. Her skirts ripped and her shoes and pantaloons burst open. And there she was on the floor for all to see; wet, disheveled, angry, and in tears.

A mermaid. From head to tail some eight feet long.

"You *swine*," she said.

"Oh, dear sweet Lord in Heaven," Ludsthorpe said. He began to fall. McTaggart got a chair under him just in time.

"You came after *me*, didn't you?" Chetwood demanded. "To get revenge on *me* for leaving you! For having the temerity to want to live with my own kind!"

"You foolish, foolish man," she said bitterly. "I came because I wished to live in England. I joined Addicock, Ludsthorpe, and Gerville because I wished to make a respectable living. And also, because you were here! Yes! I wanted to find you!"

"And take your revenge!" Chetwood thundered.

"Nothing of the sort!" she said. "You have always been a suspicious man, ready to fly into a passion at a moment's notice, but I have never been like you in that way and never shall! I have pursued you, sir, solely to inform you that the two of us, you and myself, have a son!"

About the Author

Barton Paul Levenson has a degree in physics. Happily married to poet Elizabeth Penrose, he confuses everybody by being both a born-again Christian and a liberal Democrat. He has 69 published short stories, poems, and essays. His novels *Another Century*, *Recovering Gretel* and *The Argo Incident* are available from Amazon.com.

Barton was banned from entering the Confluence Short Story Contest again after winning first prize two years in a row.

Web page: https://bartonlevenson.com/

Facebook page: https://www.facebook.com/barton.levenson/

Love and Lies

by

Melody Bowles

Love and Lies

Q uiver, foul witch! I have come seeking your fabled love potion and if you do not relinquish it at once I shall be forced to do something quite dramatic!"

Amira stood at the mouth of her latest sea cave, hooded cloak dancing in the clifftop wind, and wondered why this lordling looked quite so pleased with himself. When she didn't respond, he struck a pose with his sword, giving it a lofty whirl. When he tried to whirl it back the other way, it slipped from his grasp. A puddle of seawater splashed his pristine riding boots.

She laughed. He laughed too. Then they both remembered he was technically threatening her, so it trailed into awkward silence.

"Love potions are 99.99 per vial," she said. "Take it or leave it."

"*What* did you say?"

"99.99 or get out of my cave."

"You want…money?"

"I'm living in a cave. What do you think?"

The lordling sheathed his sword, a crinkle in his brow. "I thought you'd want…I don't know. A major organ. Or my first-born child."

"I'm afraid neither has much resale value. I want cash, upfront. You good for it or not?"

He drew a coin pouch from his belt and began the arduous task of counting one hundred coins. Amira listened to them clink against the stone and thought of the inn in Silver Lake City. A hot bath on the balcony with a glass of red and a maid to answer her every whim. Heaven.

"…One hundred," he finished, triumphantly. It took everything Amira had not to snatch up a coin and rub it against her cheek, feel the reality of the cool precious metal.

Instead, she pulled out a vial from her satchel. It was one of many identical tubes of magenta liquid, all marked with a heart symbol. The lordling's eyes shone as he reached for it, completely ignoring the penny change she held in her other hand.

"It will only work if your lady's heart is true," warned Amira. "No guarantees. And no refunds."

"How sweet you are to worry for me," he gushed. "The fair Lady Mila is the truest girl I ever met, and I plan on making her the happiest too."

"...She won't give you the time of day, will she? Or you wouldn't need the potion."

"It is true I would prefer she not call me a foolish fop of a man. Especially not to my face..."

Amira sighed. It wasn't the first time she'd heard such a story. "The potion should fix all that—if her heart is as true as you think. Good luck!"

"Thank you! You know, you are much more amiable than most other witches I've met. You didn't even try and turn me into a toad."

"Yeah, you're welcome. If anyone needs a love potion, send them my way."

Amira moved the coin into the small wooden chest she kept in her bag. The week's business has been good. Six young men and women had heard of her whereabouts and come seeking love potions. As caves liable to flooding went, this one was quite decent too. There weren't too many spiders and there was a freshwater stream to drink from. It was the perfect haunt for a witch.

As the sun set, Amira decided it was unlikely more potion seekers would come before tomorrow. She headed to the seafront. The sand was soft on her feet and the temperature pleasant. She thought about trying to fish again. Her ability with a rod was severely lacking, but her supplies were running low.

Tomorrow's problem, she decided. She went back to dreaming about her long-awaited room at the inn. There would be no smelly fish or hard bread. Only soft pastries, sumptuous cakes, and hot chocolate in a great steaming mug...

A wave drenched her to the knees. During her dreaming, she'd wandered far too close to the shoreline. As she backed away, she saw a flicker of silver light. She stopped, wondering what it was. A shadow moved beneath the sea and then rose up, water moving in a graceful arc around her. A cloud of seaweed? A dolphin? A shark? Every time she turned to get away, a wave of water blocked her path.

Then she saw her.

Amira didn't believe in mermaids. Yet she had no other word for the half-woman, half-fish that appeared before her. Her thick hair covered much of her torso, dark and shiny like seaweed. Blue eyes blinked above a delicate nose and full mouth. When she smiled at Amira, it was all teeth.

"You took my cave," she said. Her voice had an accent Amira couldn't place. Each vowel sounded too long.

Amira swallowed and tried to remember how to speak.

"I can leave. I'll go right away!"

"Humans have been coming. How do they know you're here?"

"Word gets out when you're a witch."

Amira looked at the mermaid's teeth. Perhaps she could back off towards the shore. Just to be safe.

"A witch," said the mermaid. Her eyes lit up. "I need you to get me a potion."

"A love potion? No problem. Here, take it. Free of charge as you so generously shared your cave with me."

Amira did her best to keep her hands steady as she withdrew one of the vials from her now sodden satchel. The mermaid made a displeased sound before smacking it away. It splintered against the shore with a delicate tinkle. 99.99 down the pan.

"I do not need such silly potions. I want a potion that turns me human."

"I only really do love potions—"

"Do not lie! Witches do all sorts of potions."

"Well, you see. I only do potions for people who pay. And such a potion is going to be very expensive so—"

"Are you hungry?" asked the mermaid. She stuck her face up close to Amira's. "You look hungry."

"Er. Peckish, I suppose."

"Salmon is delicious," said the mermaid. "It is easy for me to catch."

Amira gulped. "Then—then you want to trade? Salmon for the potion?"

"I find your terms acceptable," said the mermaid. "My name is Maris."

Amira's heart beat hard as she arrived back to her temporary base. The presence of the stream no longer felt like a comfort. If Maris made use of the cave, she could presumably swim in and out whenever she wanted. Perhaps Amira could block it?

But when she went to investigate, the walls of the cave narrowed too much for her to traverse them. And Amira didn't fancy going for a swim—she was soaked enough already.

So, she'd leave. But where could she go? All the rumours she'd left in her wake had been about a witch living in a cave by the sea. If she moved, her customers wouldn't be able to find her. Maybe she could leave a message in the sand. 'Witch can be found at x'. Then she let out a snort at her own stupidity. She was supposed to be the kind of witch who didn't want to be found.

Amira carefully counted her coins. Not nearly enough. She'd planned on gathering the entrance fee to the Silver Lake Sorcery Academy before arriving in the city. Her love potion scheme had been perfectly crafted and perfectly executed. Why should she have to give up on it just because some nosy, dangerous mermaid was mad enough to enlist her services?

Besides, Maris was right. She was hungry. And what did she have to lose? Maris could hardly follow her anywhere on land. As soon as she had the money, she'd leave for the city and never see the mermaid ever again.

Maris would never know Amira wasn't a real witch.

"You expect me to eat that? You've left teeth marks!"

On exiting her cave camp and heading to the seafront for a morning walk, Amira had discovered a gory pile of fish remains and Maris, looking very pleased with herself.

"I only bit off the heads."

"If you're going to dismember them, at least do it in a way that's useful. Like, maybe gut them?"

"You want to eat the guts? Is that your favourite part?"

"No! Humans don't eat fish guts!"

"Then they are missing out."

Amira let out a long, impatient breath. "How are you going to fit in with other humans if you're tucking into fish guts for breakfast?"

Maris immediately looked contrite. "You are right. I should learn the human way."

"Right. And the human way is to gut it and cook it on a fire."

Amira gathered some rocks and driftwood into a pile, then stripped some sticks to use as stakes. Maris watched her in a way that seemed interested rather than intrusive. Once Amira was done, she drew a box of matches from her satchel.

"Why don't you use the witchfire?" asked Maris.

"Wouldn't want to waste it on fish," said Amira, a little too quickly. "It makes it taste funny."

She staked the first fish and then held it in the flames. Maris leaned closer, reaching out with webbed fingers…

"Don't touch!" Amira said, smacking her hand away. "Not unless you want to end up like the fish."

It browned quickly. Amira burnt her mouth because she was so eager to eat. It tasted soft and sweet, the best thing she'd had in weeks. When she looked up, she saw Maris holding one of the other fish out on a stake. She was smiling. Without her teeth showing, she almost looked gentle.

A week passed. Amira sold more potions. Then another week. The days were filled with sunlight and gently lapping waters. She began to look forward to meals with Maris. It turned out the mermaid was quite the storyteller when she was in the right mood. She seemed to like sweeping love stories most of all, with dramatic sacrifices and grand gestures.

"Humans will do anything for love," said Maris. "It is the reason I want to leave the sea and come into your world."

"So, there aren't any mermaid love stories?"

"Any mermaid who loves a human is guaranteed to be dead by the end of the story. Stories without humans are not much better. Usually, one partner gets eaten or killed. For a mermaid, love is a dangerous thing."

Amira thought of the people who came to her, desperate for someone who didn't return their affections. Was that part of love's spell, to want what you couldn't have? People were willing to pay so much for love. It was something that never ceased to amaze her.

"It's not always safe for humans, either."

"All the same," said Maris. "The ocean is dangerous. I am more likely to end up fighting another mermaid for food than falling in love. And I think love would be nice."

"So as soon as you're human you'll start dating?"

"Dating?"

"That's how it works in the real world. You meet someone, like them, ask them on a date. That means you go to a restaurant together. Then, if you like them, you keep going on dates and it becomes a relationship. Less dramatic than the stories, but more practical."

"Hmm," said Maris, sounding rather unimpressed. "What's a restaurant?"

"People cook food for you so you can eat together."

"So even with humans it comes back to eating…"

"Sorry to disappoint."

"Have you been on many of these dates?"

"Unfortunately, you need a certain amount of money. Which is why I'm out here selling potions."

"So, you get dates by providing food. I can catch and cook fish."

"I'm sure lots of people will want to date you," said Amira. It came out more flirtatious than she intended. Maris looked pleased. Then Amira felt guilty, because she knew there was no way she'd be able to deliver the potion she'd promised. She didn't even know where to start.

An uncomfortable knot formed in her belly. She couldn't keep this up much longer. She'd soon have to leave or tell Maris the truth. Neither felt like attractive options. Life had become rather comfortable, a rarity for her.

Maybe the best thing was to enjoy it while it lasted.

Amira grinned. She'd seen a girl coming towards the cave over the crest of the hill, atop a white horse. Young, dumb, and willing to pay for love.

As Amira's mark grew closer, she frowned at what she saw. Her clothes were ordinary brown with plenty of patches. There was a sword at her hip, crafted not by an expensive blacksmith but more modest hands. Her skin was not painted and her russet hair, lovely as it was, straggled from its braid. This was no wealthy woman with money to burn. Commoners were rare customers.

"You're the witch," said the newcomer. She dismounted and drew her sword. "If you don't remove the spell I'm under, there's going to be hell to pay."

Amira laughed, trying to cover her anxiety. "I have cast no enchantment upon you. How could I? We've never even met."

"Don't play innocent. Lord Alfred told me everything. He came to you for a love potion and the foolish fop of a man used it on me."

Amira remembered the lordling with the shiny boots, dejected by a sweetheart who'd called him a fop. Great. He'd dropped her right in it. This must be Lady Mila.

"How do you know he used my potion?" Amira asked, stalling for time. She didn't like how close that sword was. Unlike the lordling, this girl looked like she knew how to use it.

"It's been driving me mad. The way I can't stop thinking about him. And I cannot, I repeat *cannot* be in love with a man who reads poetry to his horses!"

"I understand," Amira lied.

"I got tired of the same old sad poems, so I got him a book of romantic ones instead. When I gave it to him, he looked at me with big sad eyes and said he'd done a terrible thing which he'd never forgive himself for. He slipped a love potion into my tea."

"And then he told you about me."

"Damn right. So, you better undo your silly potion right this minute."

Amira nodded. "Yes. Of course. This happens all the time, actually," she babbled. "I have the antidote right here."

She took out one of her usual vials and presented it to Mila. "Free of charge."

"Oh yeah? What's in it? Rose? Firethorn?"

"It's a secret."

Mila took the vial. Popped the cork and sniffed. "My grandmother was a witch. This doesn't smell like magic. More like raspberries and blackcurrants, I'd say—"

Amira had already started running.

The only problem was, Amira didn't know where she was running *to*. She had no horse, and the nearest village was two miles. Maybe there was another cave she could hide in?

Mila was hot on her heels. "Stop right there!"

Amira swerved and headed down to the rocks. There were plenty of nooks and crannies she could hide in, or maybe she'd be able to fit through a gap too small for Mila to chase her through. There had to be something. There was always something.

As she stumbled her way across the sand, she tripped over her own ridiculous cloak. Her hair tumbled out in thick dark, curls. It became obvious she wasn't a greying witch, just a girl. A stupid girl who lied.

Amira flinched. She could hear a strange patter on the sand. When she turned towards it, a cold, webbed hand cautiously patted her face. Maris leaned over her, worried. "Witch! What are you doing?"

"She's not a witch," said Mila, having caught up. She sounded as winded as Amira felt.

"Not a witch?" said Maris. Her voice was too soft. It was terrifying.

Amira sat up. The tide was out. There was a shallow trail in the sand where Maris had dragged herself through to reach Amira's side. She made herself look at the mermaid she'd tricked, who'd come rushing from the waters for her. It was one of the hardest things she'd ever done.

"I'm sorry, Maris. I-I only wish I could make that potion for you."

"You played with me. Pretended you were going to make me human."

"One little lie to make some money turned into my whole life being a lie. I never wanted that. It just—it just seemed easier. I know what I did was unforgivable, but I was so close. So close to my dream."

Maris made a sad, choked noise. "Others of my kind said humans were cruel. I did not think this was what they meant. You pretended to be my friend."

"I want to be your friend," said Amira. "That's always been true."

"You stupid girl," said Mila. "If it was money you needed, why didn't you use the mermaid? Do you know what witches have given to get their hands on mermaid hair? Or scales? Or tears? All of them rich with magic, potent ingredients for any spell you could imagine."

Now that Mila had said it, it seemed obvious. Mermaids were creatures of magic after all. And rare, too. Amira had never thought they were real.

"We can take it back to Silver Lake City," said Mila. "Make a fortune. Then Lord Alfred could love me just fine. I'd have money, so neither of our reputations would suffer."

"You can't just take her," Amira said, appalled.

"I can. There are plenty of old fishing nets lying around here. And I'll get you whatever you want," said Mila. "A house. A maid. Clothes for the best parties in town. A meeting with our prince."

"A place at the Sorcery Academy?" asked Amira.

"Absolutely," said Mila, laughing. "Tired of being fake, hmm? Want to learn what mermaid magic can do in real potions?"

Maris scrambled back towards the sea, but the tide had gone out even further. She was clumsy and inelegant on land. Catching her in one of the abandoned nets would be no challenge at all.

"Why don't we shake on it?" said Amira.

Mila sheathed her sword and stepped forward with her hand outstretched. Amira took her hand…and kicked her in the groin, where she wore no armour. Hard.

Mila went down swearing and cursing. Amira made a grab for the sword, hoping to toss it, but Mila rolled away. She was on her feet surprisingly quickly. But Amira was fast too. The once peaceful vista of the beach whirled back and forth as she dodged swipes of the sword.

"What are you doing? We could have everything!" roared Mila.

Amira drew out her remaining vials of the love potion and hurled them as hard as she could. Mila covered her eyes to protect them from the flying shards of glass. She lurched forwards and a particularly nasty piece tore through the sole of her boot.

"You're mad," snarled Mila.

But Amira wasn't looking at her. She was watching Maris as she slipped back into the sea and swam towards the horizon.

"Don't come back," said Amira, softly.

The shining waters of Silver Lake City would remain a dream. Amira needed to get out of the area as soon as possible. There would be other schools she could go to. The money from her phoney potions would get her a ticket on a ship headed somewhere far, far away.

A loud splash in the stream made her jump. She gathered the tattered remains of her courage and the belongings within reach. Then she crept back towards the cave entrance.

"Witch!" yelled Maris. "I know you are here! Do not make me crawl again!"

Amira hesitated. But she owed Maris a warning, at least.

The stream was not deep enough. Maris was in an awkward position on her belly.

"You have to leave," said Amira. "That woman is going to hunt you."

"You could have let her have me."

"I couldn't. I care about you."

Maris considered her. "I am still cross. But I am also grateful. Thank you."

Amira took a deep breath. "I promise I'll do everything I can to find the potion you want. I'm sick of living a lie."

"Let's look for it together."

Maris held out her arms and Amira blinked before realising she wanted to embrace her. Her heart beat hard as they came together. Different species but the same warmth.

As the sun set and the night pulled in, they talked about where they would go. How they would get there. And what they would do together when Maris became human.

About the Author

Melody writes fantastical, speculative and romantic short stories (not all at once—usually!). She co-hosts The Short Story Workshop podcast. Her story 'Protector of the Throne' appeared in Noctivagant Press. She loves mythical creatures, particularly mermaids, and is fascinated by the mysteries of the sea. Her work is often inspired by fairy tales and legends. In 2021, she was selected for the National Centre for Writing's Escalator programme for upcoming writers.

Salt

by

Adrienne Wood

Salt

*N*o one else had even seen olives before, but I had grown accustomed to curious new foods and no longer thought them bizarre. I tried them first: bitter, oily flesh, but also briny. Salty as the sea, as tears. Salt. I froze, remembering.

The taste of salt was the first thing she forbade me. It would make the change easier, she had said. I avoided it. Gradually, I became accustomed to the strange, sweet flavor of the food. It no longer seemed flat and bland, but simply delicate and light. The salt of the olives brought back the pervasive savor of the ocean, though he didn't notice.

He tasted one, made a face, and, laughing, pronounced it too strong. I took a piece of bread, hoping to conceal my confusion as well as remind myself that this was the flavor I was used to.

"Have another?" he asked, passing the bowl back to me.

I shrugged and laughed. "They are not for me." Despite the bread, the savor lasted through the evening, coloring the rest of the meal.

I could not sleep that night. I felt the crust of salt on my tongue. Instead of lying in bed, I rose and walked to the far side of the cottage, overlooking the sea. Usually, I did not seek the view, but I longed to watch the waves break against the sandy shore. I wondered if I were really so fickle that one olive would put my present happiness so thoroughly out of my mind. Was it only because I had avoided salt for so long? Would the sensation fade, so that I eventually would grow to ignore it again as just one flavor among many?

She wanted me to succeed, I reminded myself. I remembered her tone as she warned me. I tried to remember the happiness I had felt just a few hours ago, but failed. Instead, I worried. I tried to make up my mind that she would not have left such a weakness in her spell. I worried about breakfast, I worried about the dawn, I worried, and I did not sleep.

In the morning I prepared for my bath. The steam rose from the tub, warming the room. I eased myself into the water and slowly let my body become used to the heat. My head against the back, my eyes closed, I floated, enjoying the uplift. The water felt impossibly silky against my skin.

I sat as the water cooled, becoming first pleasantly warm, then pleasantly cool, then even more deliciously cold. Finally, I realized that I had spent more time in the bath than I should have. Chores awaited me. I pulled the plug and allowed the water to drain away while I continued to sit, reluctant to move from my refuge.

As the water drained away, I felt my body growing heavier until I lay beached upon the bottom of the bathtub, crushed by the gravity of land-bound life. My breath came faster, my heart raced, and all my muscles contracted as I struggled to overcome the urge to escape, to swim away as fast as I could. Not run, but swim. I could almost feel the muscles of my tail preparing for my escape into the depths of the sea.

My panic only grew while I struggled to return to my human mind, to maintain an awareness of my human body. It was the body I had chosen, that I wanted more than anything else. This body allowed me to be happy.

It was not enough. Not enough to love, to be loved. Tears filled my eyes, spilled over, and sobs shook me. The salty tang of the tears jolted me once again, reminding me of the taste of the sea. I could not abide this human world, where everything was so different from the life under water.

"This exchange is no sacrifice," I had spat at the sea witch, exulting in my knowledge of the value of love and the value of the sea. I had been so eager, and so ignorant. She had offered me a choice of two totems: a dress, and a knife. I chose the dress, and thought I had been getting a bargain.

Eventually my tears ran dry. As I dressed, I tried to decide what I should do. I wondered again if I wanted only what I could not have. Would I long again for love if I were returned to the sea? I did not know. I didn't understand what I was feeling and couldn't fathom how I could even begin to. But most of all, I didn't know how I could return to life as I had lived it for so long with such naive happiness.

He noticed, of course. He did not know, however, that I pined for the sea itself. He thought I was lonely, or sick. He tried to help me feel better: he offered me companionship, care. He suggested I accompany him in his fishing boat and send messages to my family, asking them to visit the surface. He cast about desperately for something which would make me happy once again. He wondered if I just didn't love him anymore, though this last he did not speak out loud. I could see it in the way he would slide his eyes from me when I tried to hold his gaze. I would have tried to make him understand, if I could have without hurting him. But it was impossible and I did not speak.

I took to walking on the beach: hour upon hour of walking. I walked until my feet bled, and the salt on the sand made every step feel like I was walking on knives. I could not remain still though. I felt compelled to walk, trying to understand, trying to sort out how I could love both him and the sea. Which one did I love more, which one could I not live without? How could I make such a choice? Was it even mine to make? Had I not made that choice already, so long ago, in the cave of the sea witch? Would it have been no sacrifice if the love had not been equal, perhaps that was what she meant when she spoke of understanding it only later.

Some days I let my mind swim circles around those same thoughts, but other days I simply watched the ocean, watched the waves, watched the line between the sea and the sky. My mind grew blank during those days; I existed without thought, balancing on the horizon between him and the sea, not needing to plunge into either one. The equanimity of those days was a respite from the confusion in which I seemed to live ordinarily. But it did not let me return to the peaceful happiness in which I existed before I ate the olive, before I felt the bathwater drain away from me. I could not regain that peace no matter what I did or how hard I tried.

The evening of my last day of walking, a wave threw itself up the beach, soaking my legs and dress. As it receded it left a bundle of seaweed and I thought I knew what was within it. I unwrapped the seaweed to find the knife which I had examined so carelessly in the cave of the sea witch. I knew I was standing before her again: she offered the dress or the knife. Choosing the dress before had begun the spell which cut my tail into legs.

This time I looked closely at the knife. The hilt was wrapped in what felt like sharkskin, then intricately bound in flat cords. Among the bindings were two finely detailed metal ornaments, a seashell and a castle, almost too small to be seen. A small guard separated the hilt from the blade, the metal woven into a lacy pattern like the foam on ocean waves. The blade itself was flat and smooth as water on a windless day. It was honed on one side, with a groove near the other edge, running down to the tip. The metal shone, and as I held it in the light, I could see waves running the length of the blade as the metal diminished toward the sharpened edge. I could not follow the pattern, but it felt like there was a regularity beneath the apparent randomness of the waves. The metal glinted blue-green, appearing almost sandy where it grew lightest. It was remarkably beautiful: more so than I thought possible for such a simple thing.

A loud crash of thunder interrupted my thoughts and I looked up to see the sky darkened by heavy clouds. Winds beat the waves and raised them into mountains. Lightning flashed, then thunder shook everything almost simultaneously. The rain had not started yet where I stood, but I could see it a little out to sea, pouring down onto the waves. Through the flashes, I could see him running towards me. My heart beat faster; why was he coming, why now? Couldn't he just leave me to my choice?

He stopped four paces from me while I stared at him. "It's time to come inside," he shouted over the waves and wind. "Please. Whatever you're thinking, just stop for now. Come inside. This storm is too much for tonight. You can't stay out here." He walked closer to me, arms outstretched. "We can talk in the morning, if you want. But please come inside with me."

He put his hand on my arm to pull me away from the shore, and I could feel the roughness of his skin, the heat from his body. He was too close and it confused me. I wanted so much to go back with him, wanted everything to be the way it was.

The wind blew my hair around me so it swirled in front of my eyes and obscured my vision for a moment. A huge wave crashed onto the beach, high enough to soak our legs. I wavered unsteadily, as the sand moved under me, drawn out to sea by the wave. He stepped closer, putting his arm around me to steady me, his face beside mine. I looked at him, unable to speak however much I tried.

I could not live without him: the days I had spent on the beach, the rupture between us, all of it was awful. We had been so happy. If I could only recapture the easiness of what life had been like before I remembered everything. Could I start over again? I would try. I had to. I would start from the very beginning, would make up my mind to be human, fully human, in every way. I would follow her words to the letter. I would be more careful about what I ate, I would not taste salt again. I would stay away from the sea.

He saw the resolution in my eyes as I began to smile, even though I could not say anything to him, and he smiled back, knowing me well enough to understand that I had chosen him once more.

Then the waves struck again, higher, harder. My legs were soaked, my dress clinging to my body. Another wave slapped against us and we stumbled as the sand shifted again. I fell into the water, my bundle almost falling out of my hands. He froze as he was, on one knee, arms outstretched, staring at me.

The waves lifted me and I felt myself buoyant again, the saltwater supporting me, embracing me. It caressed my skin until I felt myself overcome with the sensation of saltwater flowing over and around and through me. With every beat of my heart, I felt it's flow in my veins, and I loved it more than I had ever loved him. More than I could ever love anything else. How could I have ever left it? How could I imagine that I could live without it? Immersed in the sea for the first time since I left my life before, it was as if I never left.

Except I remained human. My legs did not melt and mold together into a sleek tail, and I could not breathe beneath the water. I remained human, tied to the human world by the spell of the sea witch. Her words came back to me even as he looked at me, his face stretched and torn by horror.

"The knife can end the spell. It will come to you when you can no longer live without the sea."

How could I have misunderstood? And yet it was clear what I had to do, what I would do, to return to the sea. I could not turn my back on it again. I would leave this human body behind even if it meant I had to cut my own heart in two to do so. As it had already been torn and broken. The spell was a formality to bind me, when the cutting had already happened. He stared at me without understanding, and I began to murmur the words as I walked slowly towards him, holding the knife loosely in my hands. I could taste salt on my lips.

"I will sacrifice love for solitude, human touch for the touch of the sea, gravity for buoyancy, tears for seawater." I kissed him as the knife of the sea witch slipped between his ribs and into his heart.

I dove under the waves, swimming fast along the bottom, the silence of the sea covering the storm that beat upon the land. I did not return to the surface.

About the Author

Adrienne Wood's stories and poems have appeared in Spider, Fine Linen, Kansas City Voices, and others. She was reclusive, anti-social, and spent all day reading books way before it was cool.

Adrienne lives in Kalamazoo, Michigan with one husband, two teenagers, three dogs, two cats, and one lizard.

To find out what stories she's playing with right now, visit adriennewood.com.

The Beautiful Ladies

by

Julie McNeely-Kirwan

The Beautiful Ladies

With each passing day, the crashing of the waves against the shore seemed closer. Sometimes Bea could almost feel a mist of seawater floating down onto her face from the high casement windows. But that was to be expected, wasn't it?

"Rice, I'm here," called Bea. She rolled her wheelchair into the Museum from the ramp at the side door. Inside, the main gallery was heavily paneled with only the windows near the ceiling to give it light. The room itself was filled with tables, chairs, and cabinets all made from the same dark-stained wood, the whole of it going dry. Used to be, the room shined with wood oil and smelled of lemons.

"G'mornin', Bea."

Rice stood midway to the front door, his brow furrowed. Rice was technically the volunteer night watchman, much as he'd been once been the paid night watchman. He had no family and nowhere to go, and Bea wasn't altogether sure anyone knew his first name. His apartment was upstairs where Bea's ancient uncles used to live.

Rice turned to limp toward the front door, then looked back at her, reluctance on his face. He was a naturally secretive man, maybe with reason.

"It was restless here, last night."

Bea shot a glance upward and listened.

Sometimes there were odd noises up there, footsteps and hoarse old voices. Bea had grown up in and around the Museum, and she was used to such things. But today she heard and sensed nothing.

So, any restlessness must have been down here. Which was bad. She lowered her eyes to Rice, who nodded. He said, "I locked up. You stay that way. We'll talk later." Then he was gone, moving fast for an old man.

Each morning, at around 8 a.m., Rice left the Museum and had two beers at Bernie's. Sometimes three. That's where he was headed now. Bernie's was a comfy sort of bar, right across a wide street. It wasn't a dive bar so much as a respectable drinking establishment for the less-than-wealthy. It catered to shift workers, including cops who rolled through the narrow streets of Sea Grove at night and the security guards who watched over factories or public buildings during the dark hours. A lot of strange stories got swapped during those morning beer fests, or so Bea gathered.

She guessed this would be a three-beer morning. Rice would tell her why in his own good time. Could be it was about Jimmy Bell.

Rice's job wasn't pointless, paid or not. Once or twice a year there would be a break-in at night. Often, it was a kid, drunk or high. Sometimes it was a recent widower or one of Sea Grove's perpetually troubled souls. But the Museum's invaders had certain things in common. All were male, all were scared, and none of them seemed to know why they were breaking into a local attraction offering nothing much in the way of money or valuables.

Some complained about a noise coming from the Museum, a high trilling at night that wouldn't stop and was driving them crazy. Most recently, it was poor desperate Jimmy Bell who pried open a window, in search of he knew not what. Jimmy'd won a bunch of state medals in swimming, years ago, but then his wife died, and the drink took him, and he never could hold onto a regular job. But he'd never done anything criminal.

"My name," Jimmy had told Rice, "they keep singing my name. And other things."

Rice rarely called the police. Usually, he tried to get anyone he caught to sit down with him and talk. The older guys, like Jimmy Bell, were usually eager to talk—whatever else was going on with them, they were almost always lonely. Two weeks ago, Bea had made her morning appearance and discovered Rice and Bell chatting over coffee and eggs in what used to be the gift shop, Bell looking lost.

"Good morning," Bea had said, smiling at their would-be burglar. "Would you like the full tour?" Jimmy shook his head and shuddered.

"Place scares me now. Loved it when I was a kid. Still have that boat you gave me. But now…" Jimmy shook his head.

"Best if you don't come back," said Rice, nodding. "We're not giving you the big 86, it's just safer for you this way."

"You don't hear what they sing at me," answered Jimmy gloomily.

"I'd be hard pressed for a proper answer to that," said Rice, staring into the bottom of his mug.

Her old uncles used to "read" Bea's tea leaves and coffee dregs, seeing her with fins instead of legs and a child draped in a burnt wedding veil. Bea couldn't help but wonder what Rice was seeing, there at the bottom of his own mug.

Jimmy went home, reassured the noise would stop and sleep would come. Later, Bea had heard Rice speaking sternly in the main gallery. His voice, and only his voice, drifted from the back wall where the Beautiful Ladies were on display, making Bea think of a conversation she'd overheard years before.

"You don't have to spend your life protecting the Museum." Her father had said this to a much younger Rice.

"It's not the Museum I'm protecting," was Rice's response.

Rice knew about the condition of the cliff and how the slow creep of erosion had changed into a structural threat. Bea wouldn't have let him stay, otherwise.

"I have an engineer who says you could end up drowning like a rat," Bea had told him, grimly.

"Yeah, well I got a cardiologist who says your engineer might be wrong about that." Rice smiled wryly, like he always did, and she dropped the subject. But they both knew that with each passing day the workings of the sea cut away a little more from the base of the cliff.

Bea wasn't too worried about herself. She lived in a trailer on what was left of the parking lot. She swam like a champ, not as well as Jimmy Bell once had, but not bad, and could probably get out of the trailer if that was what she felt like doing. But she had her own not very thrilling diagnosis to contend with.

"Your next stop is assisted living," had said Dr. Cole.

Bea believed the end of the Museum would come at night. As a child she'd dreamt of the land beneath her beloved home tilting up and sliding away under a bright moon, right into Miner's Bay. She'd seen the Museum's bricks raining down, some falling inward, some falling away and exploding outward as the building collapsed. Then the cliff angled up even more acutely and the whole building slumped, as if defeated, and slid into the water, transformed in seconds from a living structure on the land into a ruin beneath the waves. In the dream, dark forms swam all about the drowned Museum, some almost seeming born from it, all of them with hair trailing and long hands and arms reaching out.

Bea was a rational person. She ignored a lot of what her father used to call "the woo hoo." But the engineer's report seemed to confirm the essentials of the dream. The Museum was doomed.

Today, however, the building remained standing, and she had work to do. Years ago, Bea decided to keep up the property and the Specimens as best she could until the end. The alternatives were to live amid decay like some old madwoman in a Gothic novel or to sell the collection. The first option was depressing and ridiculous. The second was unacceptable for a number of reasons, some of which could not be discussed in polite company.

Bea rolled through the wide aisles for her daily maintenance tour. The Museum's gallery took up most of the first floor, and that is where the collection lived, under low lights and glass. The room itself might have had the woody look and feel of an old library, but the room didn't smell like old books. Not at all. It smelled of the sea. More and more like the sea.

The Specimens were on every surface and in every nook and cranny. The smallest Specimens were in the cabinets, resting in trays with multiple slots. There were also display boxes, from shoe-sized up to trunk-sized. The display boxes rested on six large tables and featured the medium-sized exhibits. The small Specimens might have been lovely to see during a swim. The medium exhibits, most of them, might be enough to paralyze a diver with fear.

The largest and strangest Specimens, the Beautiful Ladies lay in their own glass-topped caskets against the back wall. The Ladies were the mysterious crown jewels of an already inexplicable collection. Nestled in white satin, clothed in white lace, each Lady was accompanied by the same explanatory card written up for every other Specimen. These cards included the age, origin, history and so forth for each Specimen. Their cards said the Ladies had been manufactured in 1931, for a long lost horror movie, Fatal Song. A man named Ardwin in Pasadena had created elaborate molds and cast The Beautiful Ladies using some exotic variation on tree rubber.

"Lies, all lies," her uncle Bert once said, when sodden with brandy.

The truth was, no one knew for sure where Great Grandpa Jack had found the Beautiful Ladies or who had made them. Or how. As far as Bea knew, The Ladies really were old Hollywood props.

But there were many other Specimens and, to Bea, most looked like old friends. Today's candidate for restoration was No. 25, and she was marvelously nasty to look upon.

No. 25 was a specimen with a round lamprey mouth, its rows of teeth permanently bared in a vicious and layered snarl. The creature's ears were pointy and torn, and its nose no more than a slitted bat-like bump. A single golden cornea shown in one eye hole, while the other eye hole was dark and empty. If shaken, something rattled around in its ghastly little head and Bea presumed it was the other eye. But who was to say? Another of the mermaids, always a rattler, had eventually given up a gold coin from between her lower ribs. The coin had been worth a fortune. Bea had been able to install a sprinkler system from the proceeds, along with a few "improvements" proposed by Rice.

The Fire Chief had been thrilled by the sprinkler system, on safety grounds. Every child in Sea Grove used to come through the Museum at least once in their elementary school careers. Most came two or three times. No one, Bea included, could ever explain why. A museum based on deception was, if anything, anti-educational. But still they came, the children, year after year, countless busloads of them. To be tricked. Happily, a good sprinkler system insured the children of Sea Grove were safe while the Museum eroded their grasp of science.

Only the mayor had objected to the new sprinkler system. Tucker was a distant cousin of Bea's. ("But not distant enough!" she sometimes complained.) This gave him, he felt, "certain rights as to disposition." He wanted the windfall spent not on the Museum, but on the failing cliff.

"It's for the family and the community," Mayor Tucker had announced in his most righteous tones.

It had soon come out the mayor hoped to inherit the Museum's seaside lot, thanks to some ambiguous wording in the original Trust. What he couldn't seem to grasp was that Mother Nature had already made her decision. Nothing could save the cliff, not anymore.

Nonetheless, Mayor Tucker tried to sue Bea into using her windfall, and then some, to shore up the cliffside. He also tried to use City funds to pay for the lawsuit.

The voters of Sea Grove promptly voted Tucker out in the next election, mostly for being annoying. Tucker continued to call himself "Mayor" and to insist that everyone address him as such. But the lawsuit went away.

The sprinkler system brought the Museum up to code and another cheery decade of duping students ensued. Sadly, however, the most recent engineering report meant that the only safe thing to do was to close the Museum to visitors. Dreams notwithstanding, the cliff could go at any time.

Bea decided that that, yes, it was No. 25's time for restoration. The bony neck of No. 25 hooked down into an unlikely hominid torso before ending in a lengthy curling fish tail. Most of the body was brittle and all of it needed a good dusting and a bit of patching. But not much linen would be needed. The whole piece was about the size of a big doll, with the tail giving it some length.

It was a gaff, of course. Or was it spelled "gaffe"? Twenty years ago, Bea's uncles used to squabble over the spelling. Nowadays, Bea still saw both spellings in every article her search called up. Strange. People were certain about so much these days, but they couldn't decide whether gruesome sideshow frauds should get that final "e" or not.

But, yes, Maudie was a conglomeration of salvaged bits and pieces—paper mâché skin over a plastic Halloween skeleton torso, hair from stuffed animals, eyes made of marbles. The savage little mouth was a carefully carved and painted lump of plastic. The skull, possibly, was more or less real. It came from some creature, possibly a raccoon, and was heavily modified. The stitched-on tail came from someone's catch of the day and some terrifying combination of dyes and preservatives had kept it seaweed green, although it stank a bit. One of the few acquired by her father, it needed care, but it was still newer than most of the other pretend beasties in the Museum.

The Halliwell Museum of Mermaids was over a hundred years old. It featured around 90 gaffs (or gaffes) in the form of horrifying mermaids, most of them the product of creative taxidermy, some entirely artificial. A small number couldn't be explained.

The story the family shared was that Great Grandpa Jack had taken to collecting fake mermaids the same as other people took to collecting beer cans, stamps, or pencil sharpeners. The whispered story was that the collection had a higher purpose.

"Not created in memoriam, but for the dormancy cycle. Just the cycle." These were the words of her father on his deathbed. In his last days, eyes sunken, his skin like tissue, he'd reminded Bea of a terribly delicate gaff, something to handle with gloves.

He seemed to be telling her the Museum and its collection were not intended to last forever. Never had been. It made sense. The cliff was eroding before the Museum was built, and the rose gardens slipped away early on. By now half the parking lot had disappeared into the depths.

Her ancient uncles also used to hint that Great Jack had planned it this way, that he hadn't planned for an endless legacy. He'd planned for something that came to an end. If true, Bea had no quarrel with her ancestor's thinking. Such was life. All things pass.

Bea worked away contentedly for several hours, stopping to admire her results when the rattle of keys announced Rice's return. No. 25 was dusted and a new "skin" had been laid atop holes gnawed by mice. The missing eye had been restored to its socket and the fleshy pink of its round mouth had been brightened up with paint. Once dried, it could go back in its cabinet, its awfulness renewed.

Rice came in very late, happier than when he'd gone out, and smelling of beer. Bea leaned back and made an expansive gesture.

"What do you think?" she asked.

Rice stood over No. 25 to get a closer look, making a show of cleaning his glasses first.

"It's hideous," he answered.

"Thank you," said Bea. "I certainly thought so."

They beamed at one another. Then Rice's smile dimmed, and he said what he had to say.

"It's restless here. I…I think I saw one of them move. Maybe it was a jolt from the cliff shaking, but that's just another flavor of bad news."

Bea didn't say anything, because she knew more was coming.

"Saw Jimmy on the way in, not five minutes ago. He can't make himself stay away. The singing is that fierce. Says he's been seeing Tucker driving past, over and over. In a truck. He's with someone."

Mutely they looked to one another. Bea put down No. 25 and frowned. She began to roll toward the back wall of the Museum, at last admitting to herself this had begun to be an area she avoided.

For Bea, The Beautiful Ladies existed in the Uncanny Valley or, anyway, the undersea version of it. There was a deep unrightness to them. Her scientist father had never come to peace with the Ladies either. He'd said the gap between what he saw and what he was supposed to see was a hair too wide.

Bea stopped her wheelchair an inch away from Specimen 1C, staring through the glass, feeling relief. At least 1C was still there. Still unchanged. She saw Rice checking the other caskets.

Specimen 1C, like Specimens 1A and 1B, was a master class in the term "terrible beauty." As far as she knew, Bea was the only person who could pledge there wasn't a single seam or stitch visible on any of the Ladies, from their inhumanly exquisite heads down to the magnificent, flaring fish tails covered with scales and glowing with peacock colors.

But even Bea rarely touched The Beautiful Ladies. She kept their bodies partly covered in cut lace dresses, gently tucking the cloth around the arms and torsos, changing out the lace when it yellowed. Rice always said they looked like brides. The Ladies never grew dusty, and no rodent had ever left a mark on those strange smooth skins. Bea claimed their glassed-in caskets kept them perfect, and Rice never argued the point.

In part, what made The Ladies disturbing was they seemed desiccated. Huge collapsed eyes peeked out under heavy lids, making The Ladies seem watchful. Their noses were straight, and the shape of The Ladies' lower faces hinted at powerful jaws. Their dried-out lips were drawn back to reveal oversized and peculiar teeth.

All told, each was about eight feet in length. Their skins felt, if not precisely alive, then organic. Not a hint of the human creative touch shown anywhere. They were, she told herself firmly, the best gaffs she'd ever seen.

"Let's order a pizza," Bea said.

Food came. They ate in the old gift shop and drank brandy and talked. Being old and at a loss, and out of ideas, eventually they fell asleep, Bea in her wheelchair, Rice in the comfy chair that seemed so out of place near the old cash register.

When Bea opened her eyes, the moon was shining in through the high windows, and she was gazing directly into her cousin's face. Tucker was holding a gun. In the moonlight she could see that craziness had settled into his bones.

"We are gonna fix this, Rob and me," snarled Tucker.

"How are you going to do that?" asked Rice in his friendliest tone, sitting relaxed in his nearby comfy chair.

"My pal Rob is going to create a breakwater in the front part of the cliff, leaving the rest of this nice ocean front property for me."

"And he's going to do this with…?" Again, Rice was as friendly as could be.

"I dunno. Maybe dynamite, maybe plastique. Depends on what he grabbed."

Rice turned to Bea, smiling slightly.

"Bea, it has been an honor and a privilege."

"Likewise."

Tucker began to look confused as well as crazy.

There was a noise in the main gallery, and Tucker ran toward it, seeming to forget Bea and Rice.

Rice, limping, pushed Bea out of the gift shop.

"Get in here," commanded ex-Mayor Tucker. And they went, really having nowhere else to go. Tucker was standing in the middle of the main gallery, his head swiveling, listening.

Rice slowly pushed Bea into the room and behind a cabinet. He then reached over and pulled the fire alarm as casually as he'd wave at an old friend. A huge shrieking noise filled the room and the glass tops of the caskets for The Beautiful Ladies began to open automatically as water poured from the ceiling in a ceaseless rain. Other cabinets began to open as well.

Tucker fired twice at Rice, who cried out, his leg wounded. Then Tucker turned to stare at The Ladies. Their caskets were already beginning to fill with water and the floor was ankle deep.

Stumbling over to 1C, Tucker grinned madly down into the casket.

"Aren't you pretty? I've got you now. Pretty, pretty, sing to me. You can be my toy."

Tucker reached down, the embodiment of hunger.

Bea was mostly focused on trying to tie off Rice's wound with one of her socks. But in one of her glimpses at Tucker she could have sworn she saw a slim and terrible hand rise up to grab Tucker's wrist, the hand climbing up him as he was dragged down into the casket.

The rest was screaming.

When Tucker stood up again, swaying on his feet by 1C's casket, no one, not his dearest granny, could have recognized him.

He stood there for twenty or thirty seconds, not knowing he was dead, then he dropped.

It was then that they felt the explosion more than heard it. Their world shifted, throwing Bea and Rice down into rising water. A falling motion, terrible in its way, made it clear that the Museum was off its foundation and sliding into the great deep.

The lights went out and everywhere in the water was the green glow of sea life. Bea opened her eyes beneath the water, seeking Rice, and saw into three faces that filled her with joy and horror, because she knew now the dormancy cycle had ended, and The Beautiful Ladies were returning to the sea.

"Swim," voices trilled as the Museum disintegrated.

Bea came to herself on the sidewalk across the street from Bernie's. Jimmy Bell was next to her, tending to Rice, who was coughing up a gallon or so of water from Miner's Bay.

Someone in the nearby crowd commented that a man named Rob, very drunk, had been arrested.

"They sang. They sang to me," said Jimmy Bell, uncertainly.

"Thank you, Jimmy," answered Bea.

The cliff was gone. The Museum was gone. Bea's trailer was bobbing around like a bathtub tugboat, but riding low. Yet her wheelchair sat on the new shoreline, dripping, but undamaged, waiting for her.

"Bea, Bea!" said Rice, pointing.

On the sidewalk, wrapped in wet, white lace, like that from a wedding dress, was No. 25.

About the Author

Julie McNeely-Kirwan is a stone and goes where she is kicked. Currently, she lives in Arkansas with two elderly rescue dogs. She draws and paints with more joy than skill, and loves to read speculative fiction with a funny bent. Her work has appeared in *Every Writer's Resource, Spine, Overtime, Every Day Fiction, Ellery Queen's Mystery Magazine, Sanitarium,* and *Writer's Digest's Show Us Your Shorts,* among others. She also has work slated to appear in *Flash Fiction Magazine, Five South,* and *The Bacopa Literary Review 2022* (poetry).

The Fall of Mer

by

R.S. Nevil

The Fall of Mer

Mercy watched the sun set over the bright ocean waters. Peaks of landfall crested from the sea in the distance; the main land much farther away and the Isle of the Siren the closer of the two.

Mercy watched the sun as it dipped down into the green waters surrounding her, disappearing behind its vast spread. It was her favorite time of day, a time when everything seemed to stand still. A time when even the waves seemed calmer, more peaceful. The peace would not last though. Not in these waters. And not in the darkness that would soon follow.

As the final rays of light disappeared into the distance, Mercy flipped her tail, diving back down into the murky waters below. She sped off through the waves, shifting through the currents, her powerful tail propelling her faster and faster. She sped past fish and eels, sharks and whales, the dark blue waters teaming with life as she swam.

The isle of the Miros had been home to the Mer for a thousand years, a place so populated that fisherman had once sung of them, their voices telling of the legend and beauty of her people. That had been before the Siren though. Before the uprising and the Fae. And before the battles that had cost her people everything.

It had been over a hundred years since the last battle of the land walkers, a hundred years since they had stopped being hunted.

Their scales had once been the most sought-after gem in all the sea. It was what made them so valuable, and the reason the land walkers had wanted them. Harder than any known metal, the Fae had fashioned shields and armor from their scales. Her people had been slaughtered, driven to the point of extinction to obtain such a priceless gift.

The war on her people had ended as they had taken the Siren as their Queen. The Fae no longer bothered them. They no longer killed her people for their scales. All because of a woman whose song could turn a man upon himself. And she had kept her people safe for over a hundred years now.

Mercy allowed herself to float into the archway, the ancient gateway of Mer, the city of their people, and the entrance to what lay beyond. She smiled as she took in the faces of those around her, the circle she now found herself in filled with faces she had known for hundreds of years, faces she had grown up with. Her people.

"Now that Mercy has been so kind to join us, we will finally get down to business."

The words were followed by a quick round of laughter as Marge stepped forward. The High Commander of the Mergiard nodding once to her oldest friend before turning to the others.

Mercy paid them little mind as she smiled, shrugging, her own thoughts now turning toward the meeting at hand.

"The Queen has spoken," Marge said. "The Siren has sung. And she wishes for us to persuade a group of pirates to change their course."

The words seemed to echo in her head. It was not unusual for them to deflect pirates and fisherman away from the isle. It had been their best defense against invading forces for the past hundred years.

There was something else though, something Marge was not telling them. She could see it in her friend's face.

"Only this time, we will not be diverting their course away from the island. We will be diverting their course to the island."

That was new.

The sound of uncertainty was followed by objection, several of the others raising their voices in protest. It was Mercy's voice that got through though, the sound of her words hovering over the others.

"Why are we steering them towards the isle?" she asked. "It's against our protocol."

Marge took a deep breath, letting it out before she met Mercy's stare.

"I agree," she said. "But this is the order of the Queen. For reasons unknown to us, she wants this ship."

Mercy shook her head again, lowering her gaze. She could tell that the High Commander was not happy about this. She felt just as the rest of them did. This was a mistake. But it was an order. And there was no refusing an order from the Siren.

More grumbling followed Marge's words, but it was Mercy again who spoke reason.

"The Queen has a reason for wanting this ship," she said. "And in the hundred years she has led us, she has not led us astray."

Not yet. Possibly not ever. But the sinking feeling in her gut said otherwise.

She turned back towards Marge, the other woman giving her a grateful look.

"What is our objective?" she asked, trying to make sense of it all.

"Our objective is to make the pirates come to us. To make them come towards the isle. Once they are close, the Queen will do the rest."

Mercy had seen the Queen at work. She had seen the Queen use her voice to wreck ships. She had seen her turn her voice on humans as well, forcing them to do things they did not want to. It was compulsion, the song of the Siren, and it was one she could turn on the Mer at any time.

Mercy flipped her fin, drifting along in the waters, circling the outer edge.

The others were watching her, gauging her reaction. It would not do to let them see her true feelings. She would need to keep her thoughts close at hand.

"Very well," Mercy said. "It can be done."

"It will be done," Marge corrected. "And you will be the one to lead the attack."

Mercy reigned in what she was about to say. If she was leading the mission, then it meant Marge and many of the others would not be going. It would only be her and her squad.

Still, it was a mission. And if the Queen wanted a pirate ship, then a pirate ship she would have.

"I understand," she said, nodding towards Marge. She did not wait for the other woman to reply. She turned to the other members of her squad.

"Get your things together," she said. "We will leave in twenty tide pulls."

She watched, observing the rest of her team as they got their things together. After a moment though, she set to getting her own stuff, grabbing some armor and a small dagger to arm herself with.

Others grabbed small tridents, golden forks that could be used as a dagger or a spear, and bowswith arrows made of gold filling their quiver.

The weapons were a precaution, only to be used in emergency. Only the archers would likely touch them, and only rarely would they ever fire.

Mercy prayed it would not come to that. Not for the role she was about to play. And not for the mission that was to come.

Before the attacks, many of her people had not used weapons, instead relying on the physical abilities the Sea Gods had given them. Those days were long past though. And a new world had risen in their place.

"Something about this feels off," she said. Marge was standing by her side, the High Commander looking out over the vast sea before them. "I don't like the idea of leading them here. It feels wrong."

The older woman merely shook her head.

"It is not for us to decide what is right and wrong. If the Queen tells us to do something, then we follow her orders. We have to trust her. She has never steered us wrong."

That was what bothered Mercy the most. The fact that they trusted this woman so completely. What would happen if the Queen failed them? What would happen to her people?

"Do we also follow her without question?"

Mercy had never truly trusted the Queen. She was a Siren, an ancient being who predated even the Mer. She was the woman of the isle. She held no allegiance to anyone except herself. And that bothered Mercy.

"I do not disagree with you," Marge said. "But my hands are tied. The Council will have my head if I refuse."

There was a pause. Mercy knew there was more. They were close enough that Mercy always knew when there was more.

"If things get murky," Marge said. "Do not hesitate to fall back. I do not know what the Queen's endgame is, but I do not plan to sacrifice good people in order to meet her agenda."

Mercy only nodded, the other woman turning away, the current taking her further down the gate. She could only wonder what the other woman knew. Something about this did not seem right. She knew Marge would never give her the answers though.

The thoughts continued to linger as her team began to gather.

"Everyone on me," she said. Better to get this over with than to sort through everything that could go wrong. It was one of her worst traits: overthinking situations, looking for flaws that were not there.

Once everyone had gathered round, she continued.

"The pirate ship we will be attacking is in the waters to the south," she said. "Pirates are unusually nasty humans, but are also the weak. They are not the skilled fighters of the Fae."

She held their gaze, searching each one to make sure they were listening.

"I will play the decoy. Archers, you will cover from the east and west. If anything goes wrong, you will be there to provide cover."

She gazed at her three commandos, their tridents glistening in the light of waters.

"The three of you will trail me. If I need help, I will say the code word. Otherwise, you will remain out of sight. There is no point in giving our numbers away."

Each of them nodded in understanding.

"Once the pirates are trailing me, we will allow the shifters to play their part."

She glanced towards the back of the group, towards the two Mer who held a set of hooks within their grasp. They would be in charge of making sure the ship stayed on course. Using their hooks, they would make sure the direction was right.

"We need to be sure they follow us into the waters of the Isle. If there are any issues though, break out and get out of there. There is no point in risking our lives for this mission. Is that understood?"

A chorus of confirmation and nodding filled the space.

Their plan to lure them into these waters had as much to do with protection as it did conquest. Her team would be stronger here. And if things did go bad, then they would have the Queen to fall back on.

"Does anyone have any questions?"

No one said a word. They were ready. They were as prepared as they would be.

"Then follow me."

Mercy spun, using her fin to propel herself as she sped through the waters and currents, headed for the last known location of the ship.

The note that Marge had given her was outdated by at least a few tide falls, but she should still be able to use it to track them. They would be close. Humans, for all their worthlessness, had an odd habit for being very capable of navigating the waters. Especially pirates. They had the uncanny ability to traverse through the seas despite their land walking.

Mercy was old enough to remember a time when the pirates of the south sea had been great in number. A time when they had stopped at nothing to raid and kill her people. Mer scales had been popular in those days, catching a fair price at any harbor along the shores.

That had been the worst of times, in a time where the Mer had truly been close to extinction. They had changed that in the years that followed, building a thriving and vast nation beneath the waves of the sea. But the threat still lingered.

And now, they were risking all of that. If the pirates learned of their home, they would be able to track them back to the isle.

Her doubt lingered as the ship came into view. The blackened wood giving the ship the appearance of a haunted mass floating just above the surface. Mercy knew better though. She knew the shadows played tricks on them from below, and that the ship was far from haunted. In fact, it would likely be teeming with life.

She gestured to the others, putting them into position as she watched the ship glide along the waves. It was headed straight towards them. It would not take much to steer it off course, to redirect it in the direction in which she wanted.

In fact, all she needed was…

Her head broke the surface, her eyes falling upon the looming black boat, it's wood creaking along with each dip and dive of the sea. It was something out of a story, majestic in an odd sort of way. Still, she had a mission. And that mission would most likely end with its destruction.

Mercy glanced up at it again, noting the height at which she would need to board. She would need to time this perfectly. It was a leap, but it was well within her abilities.

That was as far as she made it.

Something hard slammed into her, catching her off guard and shoving her back beneath the water.

Her whole world turned upside down as the water beneath her exploded, the tides and current of the seas becoming a turbulent mass as she tried to right herself.

What was this? What sort of sorcery…?

Her question fell away as a loud explosion echoed in the distance.

Mercy tried to right herself. She tried to get her bearings.

She tried, and failed as the waters around her tossed her back, wave after wave of heated water sending her flailing back into its depths.

When her momentum finally stopped, Mercy lay there, panting, trying desperately to understand what had just happened.

All around her explosions rang out, their sounds like drums playing in the distance.

Her gaze fell upon the ship, it's massive black mass filling her with a sense of panic. The ship was not alone. Others now graced these waters, at least ten that she could see, each of them sailing towards the isle.

The realization of what had happened settled upon her like a cold fog, clouding everything around her. It was a trap. It had all been a trap.

But how? How had they known? And why? Why after all this time we're these pirates coming after them?

Mercy found her answer in the distant thunder, the beating of the drum beginning again.

Mercy dove, shooting back down into the depths of the water, retreating and praying that it was not too late.

"Move," she called. "Retreat. It's a trap."

Her voice echoed through the waters, giving her the ability to speak with her team at great distances. Only no one replied. No one answered her call.

She stared at the ships, at the explosions still rocking the nearby waters, understanding finally dawning on her.

They were gone. All of them. Her entire team killed by these pirates and whatever sorcery they had conscripted.

Anger and sorrow coursed through her as she peered up at the boats. This had been planned. They had known exactly where the Mer would be. Their attacks had been precise and exact. There was no way around it. They had been waiting for them.

And the explosions…

It had been magic.

She could feel it now. She could feel the power coursing through the currents, controlling them, manipulating them in their unnatural way.

There was only one group who had such power, only one group who could do such a thing. They were the ones who had started all of this, the ones who had begun this war on her people.

The Fae.

The Fae had found them. And if they knew…

Another blast rocked the waters around her, the surge of energy shoving her deeper into its depths, pushing against her.

Mercy fought for control, cursing herself for not seeing it sooner. She should have known. She should have realized...

And yet, she had trusted. They all had trusted the Siren. They had trusted their Queen.

The truth hit her harder than any explosion. The betrayal of her people, the deaths of those she loved. She had to warn them. She had to warn the others.

The thought fled from her mind as the raging waters overcame her yet again. And for a moment it was all she knew; the raging rolling water, so hot and angry as it tossed her about. When it finally stopped, Mercy lay there, floating in the water, panting, her lungs desperate for the precious liquid and elements her body needed to survive.

Mercy closed her eyes, images appearing in her mind. Pictures of her people, her city destroyed. The limp, lifeless bodies of the people she loved. Her people.

She knew the truth. If she did not make it back to warn them, it would haunt her for the rest of her life. And everything she loved would be gone.

These were the thoughts that propelled her, shooting her through the water and the currents that would carry her back to Mer.

She had to make it. She did not have a choice. If she did not...

The thought sent a shiver down her spine. She could not consider it.

The Fae ships may have been fast but she was faster. If she could make it back before them, she could...

Almost as if the sea god herself had heard her prayer, the city of Mer appeared before her, its wondrous structure rising high against the ocean floors.

Only after a second glance did she realize what was happening though.

Those structures were no longer standing. They were falling, crumbling in the currents and waves of the sea.

Mercy could only stare at the destruction, the carnage that had once been her wondrous city. Horror and pain strummed through her blood, panic and anger settling somewhere near the top.

There were still people in those buildings. Her people. People she loved and cared about.

Mercy pushed herself with everything that she had, her tail whipping in big, long strides, propelling her forward. Even as she swam though, she knew it would be too late. She could see the Fae's magic as it descended upon the city. She could see the fire and hell it would rain down upon her people.

And she knew.

This was the end. The Fae had found them. For thousands of years, they had warred against them. And the Fae had finally found them.

They had won. They had destroyed Mer.

She could only watch as the magic pummeled her city, destroying it.

Somewhere in the destruction the truth settled upon her.

This was why they had been sent away. This was why the Siren had sent them on the mission. She had betrayed them. She had betrayed the entire city. And now Mercy and her people were paying the ultimate price.

Tears swept from her eyes. Tears of sorrow and pain. Tears of anger and fire. The emotions thrumming through her veins.

Her people were gone. Her city crumbling beneath the waves.

She could not let this stand. She refused to do so. There was only one thing she could do though. Only one way she could exact her revenge. Revenge for all of Mer.

It was with renewed vigor that Mercy pushed forward, fighting through the pain trying to tear her apart. She could not allow it to get the best of her though. She had to fight through it. For her people. For the city of Mer.

She could feel the day's events drain on her as she swam, could feel her body begin to tire, the long swim out into the sea and the journey home now taking its toll. Still, she fought through it, battling her body and her mind as she pushed through the fatigue, the hurt, and the anger that threatened to overwhelm her.

Only the thought of revenge kept her going, pulsing through her, driving her. Revenge for her people. Revenge against the one person responsible.

The Siren Queen.

As the isle came into view, Mercy considered all her options, going over everything she knew about the creature.

The woman had seemingly been trapped upon the island thousands of years before. And while the Mer could not go on land, neither could she go into the water. Which meant her only motivation for betrayal, had been the opportunity to escape, a chance to leave it all behind.

A slow smile crept across her lips as she understood what it meant. And she knew exactly what she needed to do. It would take some work. And she would have to time it just right. But it was the only way to make sure the Siren never left the island again.

The Siren Queen.

Mercy shook her head at the words. The woman had never been their Queen. She had been an imposter, a poser playing the role in order to get what she wanted. Her freedom. And now that she was on the cusp of that very thing, she had betrayed the Mer.

Anger rose up within her, her emotions fueling her movement. The isle grew closer, and so did her destiny. She could see it in her mind. And she knew what she must do.

As the isle approached, Mercy could make out even more of the Fae ships, part of the fleet who had destroyed her home. They too would pay for what they had done. The curse of the Siren's Island would forever stay intact.

She worked quickly, making sure to stay in the shadows. It would not do her any good to get caught. Not when so much was at stake. Even the slightest misstep would prove costly.

Slowly, she made her way closer to the isle, moving with the currents that were less likely to be noticed. The sound of voices could be heard over the tide. And the closer she got, the louder the voices became.

"…we have risen above the others. And we will free our true Queen, the one who will deliver us from this fate the so-called Queen has led us to."

So that had been the ploy, to play the same game with the Fae as she had with them. To play the savior, and gain their trust. And in the end, she would betray them just as she had the Mer.

"What of the Mer? They will not take this attack lying down. They will want their revenge. And they will seek it against the coastal Cities and villages of our people."

This voice was different. It was a voice of reason. A voice that spoke true. And yet…

"The Mer are no more. Our Queen has ensured it. We have destroyed their home. We have destroyed their city. They will not bother us anymore. The Queen has made good on her promise. She has delivered us to victory, just as she will deliver us to victory over the false Queen." The first man sang, his voice sounding like that of a prophet.

Mercy saw her opportunity. She saw her chance and took it, rising from the waters.

"The Queen will betray you…" she called, dipping back down beneath the tides before anyone could see her.

She swam, moving as fast as her fins would carry her, before popping back up a few hundred feet away.

"She will turn on you, just like she did the Mer."

Commotion came from above as Mercy ducked back beneath the surface.

"The Queen will not betray us. She is the true leader of our people. Show yourself if you think otherwise."

She smiled at the words. No doubt he had been the first one the Queen had turned.

Mercy peaked back above the water, making sure their backs were still to her.

"And how do you know she will not betray you? What proof has she given?"

She ducked back down into the water before they could turn. The ruse would not work long, just long enough for her to plant the seed. But it would work. She was sure of it.

"You spit heresy from your lips. Show yourself so that we may confront these accusations…"

"There is no need for them to show themselves," a soft voice whispered.

Mercy's blood went cold. She froze in the water, lying in wait as she pondered what the Siren would say next.

"I already know the owner of this voice. Come to me, my daughter, let me free you of your burden."

Her heart skipped a beat as the woman began to sing.

"Come to me, oh precious lands,
Oh, come to me, putty in my hands."

Mercy felt the pull of the song. She felt its command. She fought against it, desperately trying to ignore it.

But her body rejected her, acting of its own accord, dragging her back out of the water. The scaly rock of the isle dug into her skin, cutting her flesh as she tried to stop herself.

It was to no avail. The spell had taken hold. And she was no longer in control.

"Oh, come to me, my precious darling,

Come to me, and be my starling."

Panic had begun to set in. Panic and fear as she gazed across the island, staring at the woman singing the song.

"You will abide my will,

You will see it through,

And in the end, you will see the truth."

Mercy stared at the woman. She stared at the crowd of Fae, all watching as she pulled herself little by little from the water, scraping her body across the hardened ground.

As she held their gaze though, she realized one thing.

Her own fear and panic were mirrored on several of the faces within the crowd. They were confused and startled by what they were seeing. Even as she continued her slow march across the gravel.

And suddenly she knew.

Her body may not have been hers anymore, but her voice was. And she could still use it. She could still exact her revenge, but it would cost her everything.

"You see…" she called, managing the words as she gritted through the pain. Her body ached from its pull, straining against it as it scraped across the hardened stone. "Even now, she calls me against my will. What do you think she will do to you?" Her words cut off as her mouth clamped shut, the Siren continuing to sing.

"I call thee too me, over the mountaintops,

I call thee too me, through the sea."

The damage was done though. Mercy could see it in their eyes. She could see it in the way they darted back and forth between her and the Siren.

"For once the Mer is right," one of them called. "Do we really want to exchange one tyrant for another?"

A chorus of agreement went up around them. And her heart felt like it might explode.

She smiled, feeling the pull of the Siren begin to weaken as the song stopped, the woman finally understanding what Mercy had done.

That small seed of doubt was all she needed. And it had worked to perfection.

There was no point in telling them that they were all stuck here. No point in telling them they were all doomed.

She had sabotaged their boats. She had damaged them beyond repair. Even now, their crews were trying to fix them. Trying and failing.

With her goal completed, she lay her head down, the draining sun slowly taking the last of her energy.

She would die here, upon this rock. Watching as the Fae began to fight themselves, trying to free themselves.

Only there was no freedom. Not from this place. Not now.

And as she took her last breaths, Mercy knew. She would be the last of her people. The last of the Mer.

And the very last Mermaiden.

About the Author

R.S. Nevil is an avid reader and author. He mainly writes science fiction, while also dabbling in different types of short stories. From a small town in rural Georgia, writing has always been a passion of his, and he hopes to one day publish entire series. While also working his regular job, R.S. spends most of his free time reading, writing, and trying to perfect his craft, coming up with new and fantastic tales of Werewolves, Vampires, and anything else of the Supernatural sort.

Facebook: https://www.facebook.com/profile.php?id=100058560523986

The Silver Council

by

Eve Morton

The Silver Council

hey were in the middle of gathering coral flowers when Bea's scale changed colour. Seelah noticed it first. She nearly dropped the two red blossoms in her hand when she saw the silver scale on her best friend. Bubbles erupted around Seelah's mouth in a silent gasp. She touched Bea's shoulder and gestured to the spot at the tip of her tail, now shining silver and iridescent under the blinker fish's light. Bea's gills flexed in response.

The mark. She had the beginnings of the sacred scales on her. She locked eyes with Seelah who had grabbed a blinker fish for closer inspection. The blue-black colour of their normal scales seemed so much darker against the tip of silver. Though Seelah found no more silver ones in her search, they didn't need to confirm what had gone on. With one silver scale emerging, it meant the rest were soon to follow.

"Quickly," Seelah said through the underwater sign language their mermaid clan had developed. "We have to go back home. And tell everyone."

The water filled with bubbles as Seelah shot ahead. Bea paused, her heart heavy. A silver scale was sacred—but it also meant responsibility. She gazed down at the dropped coral flowers and added one of them to her hair. It was the last time, she feared, that she'd be able to do this.

At home, Bea's mother signed so frantically that only her life partner could calm her down. He grasped her hands in his own and congratulated Bea for the both of them.

"We wish your father could be here," he said. Bea's birth father had died in a boating accident shortly after her twin brothers were born. She wished her father was around too. He'd been an elder in his time period—not as sacred as the silver scales—but an elder with a lot of sway in the community cove. Perhaps he could have fought against what was surely coming next.

Seelah and her mother were also in Bea's cave. Blinker fishes swam in and out, illuminating their living space, and Seelah's dark eyes flecked with gold. She was happy for Bea. Beyond happy, it seemed. In between the bubbles and speedy retreat from the coral reef, she had talked endlessly as if Bea was already a legend, already part of the shell stories that Seelah spent her evenings reading and speaking about with her younger siblings.

"We should pack," Bea's mother said. "We have a lot of ground to cover in a very short period of time. I already see the second silver scale."

Bea glanced down. Just below where a belly button would have been, had she been fully human, was the second silver scale. She could see clearly that, as the transformation continued, the silver would form a line down her body, splitting Bea in half. Her heart panged with heaviness once again. The trip to The Silver Council Cove would take at least a day of heavy swimming. At this rate, she'd already be ready to initiate into the community. The lifetime that she had once wanted to spend with Seelah vanished before her eyes in a haze of bubbles and dropped hopes.

"Can I wear the flower there?" Bea asked.

"Of course."

"And can I take Seelah with me?"

Seelah tugged on her mother's arm. Her grin was near maniacal. She fluttered and signed as if she had never been so happy. Bea's mother was less forthcoming, but once she exchanged a series of coded hand gestures between herself and Seelah's mother, the answer was yes.

"Definitely yes," Bea's mother echoed. "But we'll have to leave in mere minutes. By the rock in three lunges."

All the parents left to go to their separate cave spots in order to pack away belongings. Bea knew she couldn't take much with her, so she followed Seelah into her room. She added shell after shell with carved in calligraphy to her satchel made from an old blowfish. She moved with just as much excitement as before, without any hint of despair.

Bea couldn't bear to crush her spirits. So, she merely perched on a rock close by and listened as Seelah rehashed her favourite stories of The Silver Council, the white lights of the initiate, and the treasures from the unknown depths. She even added a couple more stories about the vampire fishes before it was time to go.

The Silver Council were the spiritual leaders of the mermaids. While there were many different types of mermaids, all speaking with various dialects based on hand gestures or echo location like dolphins, each community had a silver sea-change as part of their lore and biology. Sometimes the scales of a mermaid would transform into something more like shattered iridescence, practically lighting up the water, once they'd reach the age of maturity. Their hair would also transform from the thick matted kind typically found on most mermaid's heads to something more effervescent and floating, forming a crown-like halo around their heads. With these changes would also come extra night vision and the ability to see into far distances.

Over many centuries, the skilled vision these mermaids possessed was then parlayed through stories and other rituals into the ability to see the future. They were often called on to consult in disputes and were often the final judges of criminal mermaids or other species who had violated water treaties or agreements. The legends about The Silver Council were numerous; in every single one, they were treated like gods and goddesses with the ability of second sight.

When they weren't consulting, they were expected to keep that tradition alive. They were to practice the art of divination, using rocks and blinker fishes to tell fortunes, and in general watch over all mermaids no matter the creed, culture, or clan. They were the night guards, living gods, and psychics rolled into one. And because they were so revered across all mermaid cultures, they were all kept in one compound in the middle of the ocean. People travelled there to see them while they spent their days in their practice.

It was this compound where Bea would live the rest of her life. No choice. No say in the matter. Her scales were silver, so she was now precious.

She had never felt more awful in her entire life.

By the time the journey came to an end, her tail was half-covered in silvery scales. Her hair had already started to form a corona around her. Her mother and step-father now treated her with a reverence and respect that she'd never felt before and that still seemed undeserved. When she was too slow in her swimming, or took too long to eat her food during a rest top, they didn't chastise. They let her get away with everything, now, because she outranked them. But she wanted to be a kid again and be scolded, even for minor discretions like littering.

Seelah was the only mermaid who seemed to treat her with respect and admiration while also still treating her like Bea. As they travelled, her arms flapped like unmoored boat motors as she tried to tell Bea as many stories about The Silver Council as possible. When Bea moped and said she didn't want to hear about those legends anymore, Seelah then talked about the adventures the two of them had had together, about the coral flowers they used to find and the games they played growing up. Bea's heart warmed, but she soon grew despondent. She didn't know how Seelah could do reminisce so casually, especially knowing that by the end of their journey, they would be torn apart.

As the rock gates of The Silver Council became visible, Bea merely tried to enjoy the company while she could.

"Welcome, welcome. We've been waiting for you," one of the sacred silver greeted. They'd just passed the rock face with the symbol for the compound carved in it. The mermaid went right to Bea and grasped her hands. "We knew you'd come to see us."

"Because we're psychic now?" Bea sighed. Her movements were jagged, signalling sarcasm. If the silver mermaid noticed, she did not give any indication of it.

"I'm Marigold. I'll see you to your room."

"What about…?"

"Your guests, as always, are welcome to stay the night before they return. Travel arrangements and other items have been prepared."

"Can…can Seelah stay with me?"

Though Marigold seemed to find this request quite odd—*guess she didn't see it coming,* Bea thought—she eventually nodded. "Of course. First nights are the most monumental. We shall all meet in the dining area when it is time for initiation."

After Bea's parents signing a profuse thank you, Marigold disappeared. Due to the size of Marigold's corona of hair, it was clear that she had been a higher-up member of The Silver Council. Others appeared soon afterwards, each with a smaller crown, in order to act as guides so everyone could be settled without fuss.

Once she and Seelah were enclosed inside the small room, Bea turned to her friend. She was already unpacking her shell-stories and trying to find the right piece of shale so she could add to them.

"I've been keeping a list of all the famous Silvers from our area," Seelah said. "I can't believe I can add your name."

The love that Bea had felt for Seelah all this time bubbled to the surface. This moment, here inside a cave, would be the last she would ever spend with her without the weight of the water—and the future—between them. She took out the coral flower that she had been wearing in her hair this entire time and placed it over the pages that Seelah had been inscribing.

"What is this?"

"Something to remember me by. Maybe even something for you to write about," Bea said. "Besides, I don't think I can wear it much longer with my hair like this."

Seelah beamed. She added the flower to her own hair. Bea was overwhelmed by the urge to join their mouths in what humans called a kiss. She and Seelah had done it before, ages ago, when she'd found human books and laughed at the act. They'd practiced it together, thinking it was a joke, but it had soon turned serious. Bea wanted that cloying, coaxing serious feeling that started in the base of her tail to overtake her once again. It would combat the overwhelming specialness she felt now. She could be different, human, or at least a normal mermaid again with Seelah next to her side as always.

Bea perched on the rock with Seelah, who suddenly caught her gaze. She smiled—but seemed to look passed her.

"Your eyes have already started to change."

"Have they?"

"Yeah. What do you see?"

"A lot. Love."

"Love? Really?"

Bea bit her lip as she nodded. When she leaned forward and pressed their mouths together, Seelah moved into the embrace. She must have remembered it from before—and she must have liked it, because she allowed the inner parts of their mouths to touch. Hands roamed over their bodies. Gills were touched with the edges of fingers, causing shudders and more bubbles between them. When Seelah touched one of the silver scales, Bea trembled. It was so much more sensitive than before.

"Did I hurt you?" Seelah asked. She shifted away.

Bea shook her head. She moved closer, wanting to experience that sensation all over again. But two blinker fish went by the opening of the room, announcing the time for dinner. And initiation.

The moment, the last one Bea thought she'd ever feel, had passed.

Initiation amounted to reading a special incantation after dinner and pledging her alliance to the Sacred Silver. Though the words sounded beautiful, and the ceremony was full of light and shimmering silver, it made Bea's heart heavy once again. She could still feel Seelah against her lips. Her hands against her scales, and her own hands against Seelah's gills. She wanted to feel that all over again. In spite of what second sight she was supposed to have in this form, she could see nothing but a big blackness of the future in front of her.

"Welcome to The Silver Council," Marigold said. She added an ammonite fossil to the top of Bea's hair, matching all the other fossils the other mermaids wore. "You are now home."

Come morning, when it was time for her family to leave, Bea had completed her transformation. She could see so much farther in the water—but again, no second sight. The future was still blank and black. She hugged each of her parents goodbye as they sung her praises. When she got to Seelah, though, Seelah seemed sadder than she ever had been.

"I'm going to miss you so much," Bea said. She held Seelah to her body longer than the standard hug. Seelah hugged back fiercely, not wanting to let go. But she didn't speak. Her sadness seemed to mute her and blunt all of her interactions. She gave a half-hearted wave before swimming away with Bea's parents.

Fifteen minutes later, when Bea looked out into the ocean, she was sure she saw Seelah look back with wonder. But as quick as the image came, it was then gone.

And her new life had begun.

Weeks passed. Bea fell in sync with her new community and learned to love her bunkmates. Jaya and Deena were both young like her, barely in their twentieth decade, and they all came from around the same area. For a few days, Bea did nothing but talk with them in their regional sign language in an attempt to ward off her homesickness. But then Marigold visited her bunk, insisting in no uncertain terms that Bea must start her training.

"I thought this was my training?" Bea asked. "Don't I sit around and wait to council? And no one has needed a council. Yet, anyway."

"Everyone always needs council. We're just not sending them to you yet because you do not know our history."

"You mean the shell-stories?" When Marigold nodded, Bea had to fight off a wave of nostalgia for Seelah. "I think I know those plenty. Don't worry about me."

"You know the rumours. Mermaids talk. But very few of them read and listen. Tita will take you to the library and our archive. I expect you to spend the rest of your time there, so you can fulfil your honour and destiny."

Bea fought the urge to mock Marigold. Instead, she bowed her head and then followed Tita to the library area. It was located in the farthest region of the compound, almost completely closed off from the living room, dining areas, consulting area, and bunks. The rock face that held the items was etched in gold and covered with the same calligraphy that Seelah had learned and practiced so often. Once they stepped inside, a dozen shimmering shells stared back at her. A pink one, located on a bottom rock, looked so familiar. When Bea swam over, she could have sworn it was the same one that Seelah had been carving into the last night she was here.

When someone brushed her arm, Bea turned to see Seelah. She gasped and bubbles surrounded her.

"Am I having a vision? Is this a vision?" Bea asked. She turned to Tita and then back to Seelah. She was still there. Her smile was bright, and her eyes were as dark as they had always been. The coral flower was still in her hair. This was Seelah. She was real. This was not a vision.

Bea wrapped her arms around her friend before she even thought about the consequences.

"What are you doing here?"

"They needed a librarian. And I noticed they were missing some key names and key texts." Seelah gestured to the pink shell. "So, I made an arrangement."

Bea couldn't believe it. Over her weeks at the compound, she'd seen non-silvered mermaids—but they were always the ones seeking council or the older mermaids who acted as chefs and hunters in order to feed them without worrying. They had mermaids that cleaned too, in order to keep The Silver Council solely focused on studying. Bea didn't even realize that others, non-silvered, could be allowed inside the sacred vault of texts.

When she realized that Seelah had had to trade every last item of shell she had ever collected in order to gain entry, it seemed like too much to pay—but Seelah seemed just as joyful to be a part of the larger legend she'd grown up studying.

"I can be a scholar now," she explained. "Not as sacred as a Silver, but still needed."

"I've never been so happy," Bea said, wrapping Seelah in another hug.

"Not even when you realized you were a Silver?"

"No. Because I thought it meant leaving you."

Seelah didn't answer. She glanced around the library, and upon realizing that Tita was now gone, placed her mouth against Bea's. The kiss turned into something more probing, something that made Bea's scales feel warm—in the best way possible—once again. When they pulled apart, they were all smiles.

"So, tell me," Seelah said. She picked up a shell and opened it up. "What's the next story I should write down?"

Bea took a seat on a rock. Her vision cascaded in front of her, second sight in full bloom. The next legend would be a love story with a happy ending, she was utterly sure of it.

About the Author

Eve Morton lives in Waterloo, Ontario, Canada with her partner and two sons. She spends the days running after those boys and the nights brainstorming her next creative project. At some point, she writes things down, usually while drinking copious amounts of coffee. Her latest novel is *The Serenity Nearby* published in 2022 by Sapphire Books. Find updates at authormorton.wordpress.com.

The Woman in the Sea

by

Lisa Trefsger

The Woman in the Sea

*H*e gazed at the horizon. The longer he stared, the greater the distance between it and him grew. The smudged line between ocean and sky blurred as night fell. Yet, he could see the difference. The sky was the color of eggplant, the ocean bluer with flecks of green and white shimmering in the darkness. He scanned the darkness again, intensely gazing at the water, and waited.

Would he see her again? Would he see her tonight? He had searched these waters for nearly three quarters of a century, only seeing her a dozen times, fifteen at most. But he knew she was there. She was always there, even when he didn't see her. She was there, just the same. He sensed it.

He was six the first time he spied her.

It had been a terrible day at school. He had been cranky, and his brothers and sister had teased him, calling him a crybaby and a pansy. He always hated that. Whatever had happened at school that day shortened his fuse, and his retorts included a few inappropriate words for a six-year-old.

At wit's end, or able to see the bomb about to explode, his mother slammed her fists on the table with the force of an exploding soda bottle. The salt and pepper shakers bounced and toppled. All conversation halted.

"Enough!" she said through gritted teeth, barely raising her voice. "George, clean up the table when everyone is finished. Thomas and I need to get some air." She then wiped her mouth with her napkin, tossed it over her plate, and stood. Thomas knew enough, even at that age, to follow his mother's lead. He followed her into the hall where they donned their jackets and headed out into the dusk.

They walked down the pier, across the beach, and along the water's edge, neither saying much. She was contemplative; he was waiting for his punishment. At the jetty, his mother stopped, lowered herself into a cross-legged position, and patted the cold damp sand next to her. He sat and followed her gaze. She was watching the ocean, scanning the sea, searching for something. But what, he couldn't fathom.

His father's family had been fishermen as far back as they could trace, possibly descended from the original Vikings that had used the island as a fishing camp. His mother's family, however, was a mystery. She was raised by a sea captain and his wife who found her in wreckage after a storm. There were no other survivors. They assumed she had been birthed at sea during, or just before, the storm. Despite her harrowing start, she, like her son, had always been drawn to the sea.

As he sat there, pondering his punishment, wondering what his mother had in mind, Thomas lost himself in the undulating motion of the waves. The pounding surf had always hypnotized him. He closed his eyes and listened to the melody created by the ebb and flow of the tide. He swayed gently to the sound.

His mother's voice broke over the rhythm, her cadence matching the tempo of the waves as she spoke. "I'm sorry, Thomas. Of all my children, you have too much ocean in your blood. I had hoped none of you would be subjected to its force, beauty, calm, and rage, as I have." She sighed and shook her head. "It will always pull you, tug you towards it. It will wear away at your soul. But it will also restore and build you up. It will buoy you like the ships that traverse it," she said.

Through the dim dark of the moonless twilight, she pointed to the farthest edge of the jetty. Peering at the space to which she pointed, he sensed the motion more than saw it. There, between the gloaming and the water's edge, he saw her; the woman of the sea, bare shoulders exposed, a pool of dark hair encircling her in the inky water.

The ocean was blue and green, with oily sheens of grey and white, all swirling into a black unlike that of the purple-black night sky. Her hair was yet another shade of black, discernable against the darkness of the sea and sky. He never could adequately describe the sight, but he never forgot it either. This black-haired mythical woman of the sea. Mermaid. Selkie. Siren. Nymph. Sprite. Naiad. Serpent. Merrow. None of them quite fit her. To him, she was simply the woman in the sea, and from that moment on, she had haunted him.

As he sat there, he sensed his mother's calm. He felt her relax as tranquility permeated the air surrounding them. His mother seemed comfortable, at home in a way he couldn't explain. "She will wait. Your life is but a season to her," his mother whispered. Unable to comprehend, he sat motionless, waiting for his mother to explain, waiting for the woman in the sea to do something, waiting for some sort of signal. The pair sat together in silence.

Over the years, he may have embellished this memory. It may have been mere minutes, but it felt much longer. Suddenly, the woman in the sea dove and disappeared into the inky water. Waves and eddies replaced her in a flash, leaving no evidence of her appearance. He blinked, squinted, peering at the place she had been. His mother sighed and stood, signaling it was time to return to their home.

This after dinner excursion became their ritual, neither ever mentioning the woman in the sea. They talked about school, errands, family, and life. They rarely missed a night. On blustery, frigid days, they would sit on a bench on the pier for a few moments, the cold sea-spray stinging their cheeks and freezing off the day's troubles. During the warm summer months, the walks took longer, a respite from the heat of the day as they combed the beach for sea glass. School functions, friends, and girls eventually took time away from the evening walks with his mother. Still, they rarely missed more than an evening at a time. Until college.

He was the only sibling that went to college. Both his brothers began working at the fishery as soon as they were of age. His sister, too, being a brilliant high school mathematician, landed one of the coveted office jobs. His parents were so proud of her, a working woman! Back then, it had been almost scandalous.

He called home frequently—until the phone bill proved cost prohibitive. Then he took to writing daily and mailing weekly letters home. His mother kept their nightly habit, walking solo each evening along the shoreline. She said it calmed her nerves and restored her soul. His father thought it nonsense, but never asked her to quit.

His father died suddenly of a heart attack during Thomas' senior year. He almost left school, but his sister, married by then, had scolded him for even thinking about it. The family had made too many sacrifices to send him to college. Dropping out would have been an insult to the family. His mother agreed. They held the memorial over Christmas, so he could take part and his sister helped their mother with the legal and financial details.

After graduation, he returned home, and he and his mother resumed their nightly habit. After work, he would stop by, and the two of them walked along the shore. He often found his mother waiting on the porch for him. She treasured their time together, but after his father's death, she tired more easily, and their walks grew shorter. Sometimes they simply sat on the pier, gazing longingly at the water. Other times, they only made it as far as the jetty where he'd first spied the woman in the sea.

The sight of the woman in the sea always brought a smile to his mother's face. Once, his mother even waved, as if greeting a long-lost friend, and the woman in the sea waved back. He never had the courage to acknowledge her like that. Still, neither of them ever mentioned her, not to each other or anyone else. The woman in the sea was an unspoken secret between them, as if speaking of her would chase her away.

Once, when he was in high school, he brought his sweetheart to the beach for a moonlight stroll. He had really liked the girl, but now he couldn't even remember her name. They held hands and walked to the jetty. As they gazed at the ocean, with giddy smiles plastered on their faces, the girl had rested her head on his shoulder. She had smelled of vanilla. He closed his eyes and when he opened them, the woman in the sea was there, closer than ever before, but still beyond the jetty. Addled, he abruptly said it was time to go and took the girl home.

He never understood what he found unsettling about that night, and why he never mentioned the encounter to his mother. It wasn't the only time he saw the woman in the sea when his mother wasn't with him, but none of the other encounters had left him feeling uneasy and questioning things. Somehow, that episode, being there with a date, had felt wrong, as if the woman in the sea had been judging or scolding him.

The woman in the sea made an appearance the night he proposed to Rosalyn as well. He wasn't sure why he thought the beach would be an appropriate place, perhaps because he spent so much time contemplating life and their future while walking the shore. As they stepped from the pier, he told her about that first walk with his mother, and how it became a ritual. He even told her about the woman in the sea. Rose laughed it off as the imaginings of a young child and the encouragement of his whimsical mother.

That night, as he stood before the jetty, his heart raced. He wasn't sure if he was nervous about Rose's answer or receiving approval from the woman in the sea as his memory flashed to the episode in high school. He worried needlessly. Rose said yes. When the woman in sea appeared, she darted about, more active than he had ever seen her, and dove below the surface with a flourish. Rose only saw a whale's spout, which made her giddy, since she believed it to be a good omen.

During their courtship and marriage, Thomas had continued his evening walks with his mother. Rose grew accustomed to delaying their meals, late arrivals, and holding a seat while she waited for her husband's return. Yet she never resented her mother-in-law; the woman never overstayed her welcome when she visited nor criticized Rose's housekeeping, cooking, or child rearing. She always brought exactly what she said she would to holiday meals, no more, no less, and was always available during emergencies.

As Thomas' mother grew weary of life and could no longer walk, he would push her wheelchair to the edge of the pier and the two of them would sit there, quietly, as the salt air filled their lungs and stuck to their skin. She made him promise to return her to the sea, to spread her ashes near the jetty. And he did. The woman in the sea was there that evening, too, as if she knew. She bobbed in the waves as he wept and emptied the urn into the surf. A doleful keening sounded on the ocean breeze that night.

After his mother's death, he had often asked Rose and his children to join him on his evening walks, but they always declined. By then, they understood it was his ritual, his private journey.

The woman in the sea had continued making random appearances, and he had continued doubting her existence, making excuses each time she appeared. Trick of the light. Power of suggestion. Overactive imagination. Mirage. Shadows cast by a passing school of fish or a whale. Dreams.

She appeared when his oldest got sick and had to go to the city hospital, when the hurricane tore the roof from his home, when his oldest brother died, and after Rose's funeral. Her appearance marked many of his life's events, but not all.

Now, years later, decades later, he was still searching for her. Still gazing past the battered wave and weather worn, ragged jetty. He wondered why. Why did he bother? What hope did it bring? What good did it do? What was the point?

Tonight, he had a different question, one he should have asked years ago. Who was she?

The salty breeze whispered to him in his mother's voice. "She will wait. Your life is but a season to her," it said.

The woman in the sea appeared. He could see her smiling. He had never been near enough to see her facial features. She was beautiful. He screwed his eyes shut, not wanting to look at her. She wasn't real. She couldn't be real.

"She will wait," the wind said again.

The waves ebbed, crashed, called to him. Thomas. Thomas. Thomas. They pounded out his name with each crash against the sand. He listened to their melody. The music of the sea enveloped him. His soul soared.

Bystanders—lovers hidden beneath the pier, late night beachcombers, a few teenagers walking home from their concession jobs—no one had an explanation. Every one of them told the same tale, without variation, confounding the police.

An elderly man swayed on the beach in time with crashing waves. Fully clothed, carrying his sandals in one hand, he walked into the surf, never flinching, backing up, or being knocked over by the waves. He just kept walking. The water reached his knees, his thighs, his stomach. He continued to move deeper.

A few of them had screamed, yelled, and even threw a shoe at him. But he never turned around or acknowledged them. Surfers were wary of the risk; he was too close to the jetty, and the night was moonless. They stood by, helpless, cautious of the deadly eddies.

The water reached his chest, his shoulders. He continued moving towards the horizon until the water covered him completely.

They panicked and paced, waiting for the emergency crews, waiting until his battered body drifted close enough to be rescued. But by then it was too late. He had joined the woman in the sea.

About the Author

Much to the consternation of her teachers, parents, and grandfather, Lisa struggled to pass spelling and grammar tests in school despite being an avid reader. When she entered college, thanks to a new thing called the internet, the future of journalism, library sciences, and the written word in physical book format, was nail-bitingly uncertain. Unable to decide what to do with an English degree and knowing teaching wasn't for her, she opted for a degree in communications with an English minor.

After years in marketing and customer service, Lisa now spends her time managing her own business, scribbling in spiral bound notebooks, and trying to keep up with her husband.

She still can't spell or pass a grammar test.

Her website is lisatrefsger.com

Mermaid's End

by

James Fitzsimmons

Mermaid's End

hich human should I be? Fiona thought.

Sitting before the mirror on her vanity, Fiona perused the personal belongings she'd filched from three lifeless bodies trapped in a shipwreck on the ocean floor: a pendant from an old woman, earrings from a young woman, a pony tailer from a little girl. A family lost in a storm. Yesterday, Fiona had put on the old woman's pendant and appeared to the lone survivor of the shipwreck, a distraught man gazing out to sea on a pier. Fiona had relished the man's reaction: "Mother! Mother! Is it you! Mother, come back!"

Donning a human's personal effects to appear as the human was a trick mermaids had played on land dwellers for ages. The illusion vanished when Fiona had leaped back into the water, leaving the man crying on the pier.

As Fiona mused over the man's grief, Tiki floated to Fiona's vanity and hovered next to her, arms crossed.

Fiona grimaced. "You just enter anyone's home when you want, Tiki?"

"A cousin may enter another cousin's home unannounced, Fiona. At least, you used to think so. You haven't returned that jewelry to the shipwreck."

"This isn't your business, Tiki."

"It is when the Headmatron warns us to leave humans alone."

"The Headmatron loves to lecture during breakfast."

"What you're doing is cruel, Fiona."

"Humans abuse our world every day. They're careless beasts."

"I know your family was—" Tiki stopped and looked away.

"Say it, Tiki, when my family was killed by a drunken fool with a spear gun and a speed boat." She stroked the gash on her tailfin, finally starting to fade, where the propellor had grazed her as she'd scampered away.

"But this human's done nothing to you," Tiki said.

Fiona smirked. "One of his kind did. So, what if I have a little fun with him. Besides, the maids in Kelp Harbor swim up to cargo ships all the time and entice merchant marines."

"The Headmatron disapproves of that too. Please, Fiona, stop this."

Fiona picked up the earrings that had adorned the young woman, clipped them on, and smiled at Tiki.

Tiki scowled and swam off.

Fiona preened in the mirror, her face taking on the woman's appearance. *Might this have been his wife? Might I be as beautiful as she?*

Fiona exited her home and swam toward shore. As she neared the pier, she saw the man leaning on a rail, peering out to sea with a face frozen in pain, pining. She pulled herself onto a jetty, her tailfin becoming legs and feet, and walked along the jetty toward the pier.

Now the man saw her in the moonlight, his imagination filling in the pieces to form a complete image. "Ruth! Ruth!" he screamed. He started panting and climbed up on the rail of the pier. Afraid he would fall, Fiona quickly dove back into the harbor and, through murky water, saw the man step off the rail back onto the pier and put his head in his hands. *The human is inconsolable*, she admitted.

She swam back to the village, to the home where she lived alone. Drowsy, she lay down but winced when an earring pushed into her ear. She unclipped the earrings, set them on the vanity, and slept.

The next day, Fiona arrived late to the breakfast hall, the morning meal already having commenced. She swam to an empty table where she started in on fresh seaweed and slug.

The Headmatron, hefty in a flowing robe and sitting on a huge cowrie shell, was addressing the assemblage. ". . . you needn't involve yourselves in the lives of humans, our distant brothers and sisters. Stay under the sea. This is your home. You've all heard that Stella of Shrimp Cove fell in love with a human and gave him her life force."

As a murmur rippled through the hall, Fiona thought of the life force that a mermaid can breathe into a human, bringing the human back to life, and sacrificing herself if she gave too much force away. Stella wasn't the first maid to fall for a seaman.

"Stella's memorial will be held after today's chores," the Headmatron continued. "According to legend, essences of the maid and the human exchange during the gift of life force, but since the maid usually dies, no one knows for sure. Best we all stick to our life here and do our daily duties: harvesting seaweed, collecting sea cucumbers, cleaning slugs, tuning the pipes of the water organ . . ."

As the Headmatron droned on, Fiona rolled her eyes and saw Tiki float to a stool next to her. "You keep sneaking up on me, Tiki."

"Have you finished teasing the human?"

"He's very distressed. Probably I should leave him be."

"You're not going to . . . give him your life force."

Fiona shook her head. "I'm not in love with him, Tiki."

Later, after Fiona had completed her chores of cleaning barnacles off statuary in the village square, she attended Stella's service and went home to the bedroom she once shared with her sister. She'd moved into a den after her sister's death but would wander into the bedroom to reminisce. Fiona grieved deeply for her parents but turned bitter that her little sister—just eight—had not been spared.

Memories overwhelmed Fiona as she looked around the bedroom at blue, green, and red tubes of twisted coral she and her sister had collected during family trips to a reef. On the floor of the room, nestled alone on sand, lay a nautilus shell. She swam to the shell and lifted it gently to her ear. The shell contained singing and laughing from their last trip. Her mother would lead the group in song, and her father would try to follow along on a conch shell. She could hear her sister singing in high soprano, and then the two of them giggling, telling their father he was off key. The sounds were faint, as nautilus shells could not retain sounds forever, and Fiona knew this nautilus would be just another shell in a while.

She set the shell down and swam to her vanity in the den. She picked up the pony tailer that had belonged to the little human girl in the shipwreck. The girl must have been of similar age as her sister.

She told herself she would not appear as the girl to the man, but after a moment, found herself twirling her long hair into a ponytail and securing it with the elastic band. She swam to the pier, heart pounding, and spotted the man, as usual, staring out to sea. She climbed onto the jetty and walked toward him.

The man's face exploded in astonishment, and he leaped over the railing. "Eloise!" He landed on the jetty and grabbed his foot with a shriek.

Fiona leaped into the water, and the man did the same. Fiona saw the man thrashing, trying to kick with his injured foot. He struggled to tread water, then went limp. Fiona tugged him to the jetty and dragged him onto rocks. She looked down at his face, handsome with a firm, square jaw, full eyebrows, and long, feminine eyelashes. She briefly wondered if she needed to share her life force with him when he suddenly came to, arms flailing. He grabbed her ponytail, and the pony tailer slid off in his hand. When their eyes met, she knew he saw her true appearance, and she swam away.

The next day, Fiona had no appetite for breakfast and would not talk to Tiki when her cousin asked if she was feeling sick. In her mind, Fiona kept seeing images of astonishment on the man's face. She imagined the man squeezing the pony tailer in his hand and holding it to his cheek. She moped around her home, thinking about her sister and parents.

She swam to the sight of the shipwreck, some kilometers from the village, in water very deep and cold. She shivered and knew she could not tolerate the cold long. She found the three bodies lying where she had found them days ago, after news of a storm and shipwrecks had reached the village. The old woman had been severely mangled by the accident, and the young woman had been gnawed on by sea creatures. But the little girl, hidden in a cabin of the ship, was well preserved. If not too much time had passed, Fiona thought it possible that she could bring the little girl back to life.

Fiona scooped the girl into her arms and hurried to the pier. She saw the man sitting on the jetty, his foot now in a cast, crutches beside him. She swam a few meters down the jetty, out of sight of the man, and lifted the girl out of the water. She opened the girl's jaw and blew into her mouth. The girl opened her eyes, her skin suddenly becoming warm, heart beating. Fiona felt energy exit her own body. The girl's eyes closed, and Fiona blew again into the girl's mouth. Now the girl remained awake, and Fiona was able to stand her up. Disoriented, the girl was turning in circles, and Fiona pointed to the man down the jetty. Fiona gave the girl a firm push, and the girl started walking toward the man. Exhausted, Fiona slid into the water.

Soon, the girl was running, yelling, "Daddy! Daddy!"

The man looked up, his face breaking into smile, and yelled, "Eloise!" He stood and hobbled toward her. When they met, he fell to his knees and enveloped the girl in his arms. "Eloise! Eloise!"

Watching from the water, Fiona had swum along the jetty as the girl ran. Fiona raised her head out of the water, and her gaze met the man's. They looked at each other, a combination of wonder and disbelief on the man's face. The man's face turned blurry as Fiona started feeling faint.

Fiona swam off, trying to make the little cove outside the village where her family lay buried. She reached the village but, unable to swim further, stopped pumping her tailfin and floated down, coming to rest on a coral bench in the square. She felt jubilation from the connection she now shared with the man through his little girl, and she sensed the love the girl had for the man.

As she looked around at the statues in the square, noticing she'd missed a barnacle on one of them, mermaids swarmed around her. She caught a glimpse of Tiki approaching fast, frantically beating the water. She smiled as Tiki lifted her off the bench and cradled her. She could see a look of resignment on Tiki's face.

"It's beautiful," Fiona said, "the little girl's name is Eloise."

Then Fiona exhaled and closed her eyes.

Mermaid's End

About the Author

James Fitzsimmons writes sf, fantasy, and horror, and his fiction can be found in *Bards and Sages Quarterly*, the *Six Guns Straight from Hell 3* anthology, and on the *Cast of Wonders* podcast.

He works in IT and says that writing a computer program is much like writing a horror story, especially when users scream.

James lives in Long Beach, CA with his family and pet rabbit, Alice Cooper.

Links to James's fiction can be found on his LinkedIn page at: https://www.linkedin.com/in/james-fitzsimmons-064ba150

Additional Copyright Information